EASY TO LOVE

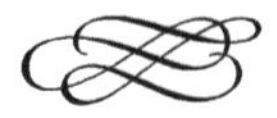

KAY SHANEE

B. LOVE PUBLICATIONS

BLP

Visit bit.ly/readBLP to join our mailing list!

B. Love Publications - where Authors celebrate black men, black women, and black love.
To submit a manuscript for consideration, email your first three chapters to blovepublications@gmail.com with SUBMISSION as the subject.

Let's connect on social media!
Facebook - B. Love Publications
Twitter - @blovepub
Instagram - @blovepublications

ABOUT THE AUTHOR

Kay is a forty-something wife and mother, born and raised in the Midwest. During the day, she is a high school teacher and track coach. In her free time, she enjoys spending time with her family and friends. Her favorite pastime is reading and writing romance novels about the DOPENESS of BLACK LOVE.

SYNOPSIS

MyLynn's Bedroom Boutique is known for the love it lends to boudoirs all over the globe. Co-owner Myla Abbott could use a dose of her own, although she'd never admit to it. While on a trip to Belize, Myla aimed to surprise her best friend by reuniting her with the lover her heart yearned for. To Myla's surprise, she returned home with a gift of her own... she's pregnant.

Kolby Ross wanted nothing to do with commitment. Confident and honest, he put his cards on the table before he and Myla Abbott engaged in the fire of passion their bodies couldn't deny. However, after spending a week with the vivacious Myla wrapped in his arms, he found himself contemplating forever.

Can an unplanned pregnancy lead to an undeniable love? Or will reality burn fantasies to ashes?

This book is a spin-off of "Since the Day We Met." Although the stories can be read separately, you may have a more pleasurable reading experience if you read the aforementioned book.

PROLOGUE

Myla Abbott

"Damn, I didn't realize how fine Kolby was," I whispered to Jaelynn.

"Kamden fine as hell, too. I could get into some real trouble with him. I may have to keep him at arm's length."

"I wonder what their parents look like because they sure as hell made some fine-ass babies."

"All three of their asses just fine for no damn reason," Jaelynn added.

Jaelynn and Braelynn were sisters, and my best friends. For the past several months, Jaelynn and I had been plotting and planning behind Braelynn's back. A year ago, Braelynn met and fell in love with Kyree, but circumstances wouldn't allow them to be together. Aside from the fact that they were in a long-term relationship, they also lived thousands of miles away from each other.

Kyree, who was from Chicago, was in Seattle for an automotive convention. Braelynn was at the same convention, but they met while she attended a wedding at the hotel, he was staying in. Sparks flew immediately, and turned into love at first sight, but didn't go beyond their one-night stand.

Jaelynn and I have had to listen to Braelynn whine about missing a man she only had one encounter with; we also had to watch her suffer in a relationship with a man that was not worthy of her. We finally decided to do something about it, and hooked up with Kyree's brothers, Kolby and Kamden, through Instagram DM's.

It took some work, but it was all worth it to see Braelynn and Kyree reunited. The love between them was palpable and I was so happy for my best friend. It's not often that you find your soul mate.

We rented a townhouse at the beautiful *Mahogany Bay Resort and Beach Club* in Belize. It was the most beautiful and romantic place I'd ever been and the perfect place for them to be reunited.

"What are you wearing?" I asked Jaelynn

We were in the room that we'd be sharing for the week, digging through our suitcases, trying to find something to wear to a club that they guys had heard about. They arrived at the resort a few hours before we did so they'd been out mingling.

"It's hot as hell, so not a lot."

I ended up choosing a short, flowy red dress that I could wear with my flat gold sandals. It was definitely too hot for too many clothes. Jaelynn decided on a pair of booty shorts, a graphic cropped T-shirt, and a pair of flat black sandals. Once we were showered and dressed, we went to the living room where Kolby and Kamden were waiting.

"Damn!" I heard Kolby say. "You look good as hell."

I smiled before replying with, "Thank you. You're looking pretty handsome yourself. You trying to find a cutie to take you back to her room."

He licked his lips, as his eyes roamed the length of my body. "I think I already found her," he said.

Suddenly, I felt hot all over and began to fan myself.

"Anybody thirsty?" I asked, going to the fridge.

The water bottles were at the bottom and when I bent over to get one, I heard, "Shit, girl."

I'd forgotten how short my dress was, and quickly stood back up. When I turned around, Kolby still had his eyes on me, licking his sexy-ass lips. Nigga had my stomach doing flips. Maybe it was the nose ring, or the tattoos that he had covering his peanut butter-colored neck and one full arm. It could have been his sexy mouth filled with teeth that could pass for dentures, because they were so straight. I also liked the fact that he was an accountant but had this thug appeal that made my nipples hard and my panties wet. *Damn!*

"Does anybody want a water?" I repeated.

Each of them did, so this time, when I bent over, I turned my ass toward the cabinets. After grabbing four waters, I closed the refrigerator door. I gave them the waters and sat on the couch, then Kolby sat down next to me.

Why is he fucking with me?

Kamden and Jaelynn sat on the couch and we conversed while we waited for Braelynn and Kyree. We had no idea where they were or when they would be back, but decided we'd wait a little while to see if they wanted to go out with us. The four of us communicated a lot through a group text message that we'd set up when we began planning the trip. There were also a few FaceTime calls, so there was some familiarity among us, although this sexual tension was new.

We heard something bump against the door and assumed it was the two lovebirds. When they didn't come in after a few minutes, Jaelynn went to the door and pulled it open.

"Are y'all gon' stand out here all night playing kissy-face?" she said before walking away, leaving the door open.

When Braelynn and Kyree came into view, they looked at the four of us with smirks on their faces.

"Y'all looking mighty cozy," Braelynn said.

I looked around and it did look as if we had paired off into couples.

"Girl, hush. You left us to fend for ourselves, so we fending for ourselves," I replied, winking at Kolby.

"Is that right?" she teased. "Let me find out y'all—" Braelynn began before Jaelynn cut her off.

"Nope! We just chillin', sis. We'll be here a week, so we're just getting to know our housemates."

"What are y'all about to get into?" Kyree asked.

"Going to that club we heard about earlier," Kamden answered.

"Word? Baby, you feel like hittin' the club?" he asked Braelynn.

"Are y'all leaving right now?" Braelynn asked.

"We can wait for y'all to get ready," Kolby offered.

"But don't go in that room and get to fuckin'. We ain't got time for all that," Jaelynn added.

"Girl! Shut up! Ain't nobody—" Braelynn started.

"Don't even tune your mouth up to tell that lie, sis. Why do you think we were gone when y'all finally came up for air?"

The whole room went up in laughter, and an embarrassed Braelynn ran to their room. She knows damn well they were loud as hell.

About an hour and a half later, we were at *Jaguars Temple Night Club*. It was a nice looking club with plenty of room, and the DJ played music for the diverse crowd of tourists. My girls and I danced with each other, while the guys stayed at the table with their drinks in hand.

"Kyree's brothers are fine, too," Braelynn said.

"Jae and I already had this discussion."

"They look like they feeling y'all."

"Kolby is definitely feeling My. He could hardly take his eyes off her back at the house," Jaelynn said.

Kolby's eyes had been on me all evening. It was already hot and the added heat from his gaze wasn't helping at all.

"What about you and Kam?" Braelynn asked.

"He's cool. Not sure I want to go there with him, though. Seem like the kinda nigga that I could fall in love with. After all that shit with Drake, I ain't ready for all that," Jaelynn confessed.

Jaelynn had a bad break-up with her ex earlier this year, so she'd been steering clear of the dating scene. She was the baby of the bunch at twenty-six, to me and Braelynn's almost-thirty. I could definitely understand where Jaelynn was coming from. At her age, I'd just ended a relationship. Chase and I dated for five years and I thought we would get married one day...everyone did.

One morning, we woke up after a night of the most passionate sex we'd ever had, and he said he loved me, but wasn't ready for the type of commitment we had. Mind you, we'd already been in a relationship for five years. Of course, I was devastated, but I wasn't in the business of trying to keep a man that didn't want to be kept. I was heartbroken, I let him go and I've been single and celibate ever since. The celibacy wasn't necessarily intentional but I hadn't dated anyone that I connected with on that level. I haven't seen Chase since he picked up all of his belongings from my old apartment a few days after he ended things.

"All three of them niggas are fall-in-loveable. You see what happened to this one right here."

I pointed to Braelynn. She was head-over-heels in love with Kyree after one night.

"Well, if they are anything like their big brother, good luck resisting them," she laughed, as another song came on for us to twerk to.

We were really enjoying ourselves. The music was great and the vibe was sexy. When the three of us heard the beat drop to "Tambourine" by Eve, we almost lost it. That song came out when Braelynn and I were about fifteen or sixteen and Jaelynn was about thirteen. We made a whole routine to it, and every time we heard it, we did it. Tonight, was no different.

We were deep into our routine when I felt some hands underneath my armpits pulling me up mid-split. I looked behind me and it was Kolby, pulling me off the dance floor. I was so shocked that I didn't react until we got back to the table.

"What the hell is your problem?" I yelled in Kolby's face.

"What was all that?" he asked, flailing his arm towards the dance floor.

"I was dancing."

"Myla, did you forget you're wearing this short-ass dress? Your whole ass was out."

Oh...I guess he did have a point.

"Why are you worried about it? I ain't your woman."

"That's not the point. We came here together, so we together."

I cocked my head to the side and folded my arms across my chest. I didn't know what he meant by that, so I decided to test the waters.

"When we leave the club, are we still together?" I asked.

"If you want to be."

Whew, Jesus. The heat that radiated between my legs could have started a fire.

"Okay."

The rest of the time at the club, we stayed connected. Whether it was his hands on my waist or an arm around my shoulder, he didn't let me out of his sight. By the time we went back to the townhouse, I wanted to fuck him from here, to moon and back.

Throwing caution to the wind, I pulled Jaelynn to the side and asked if she could sleep in the room with Kamden. If looks could kill, I'd be dead. I was a little tipsy so I giggled at her reaction.

"My, you saw us arguing damn near the whole night. He might kill me in my sleep."

"Girl, hush. He ain't gon' do nothing."

"You lucky I love you, and know how much you need somebody to knock the cobwebs off that pussy."

I gasped. "Shut up!"

Although she was right, I didn't need to be reminded that I hadn't had sex in three years.

Braelynn and Kyree had already gone to their room. Jaelynn went to the room we shared and got what she needed for the night. Kamden didn't seem to mind that she was staying with him. It wasn't like they had to sleep together, because the room had twin beds. Kolby got what he needed from their room and we said our goodnights.

He closed and locked the door behind him and sat next to me at the foot of the bed. His hand went to my exposed thigh and he squeezed.

"You good?" he asked.

"Good and horny."

"Damn! It's like that."

I nodded. "Just like that."

"You know we'll be here all week. We don't have to do this tonight. You've been drinking and—"

"And I know exactly what I'm doing. I'm not drunk."

He stood and turned to face me, then pulled me to my feet. At the club, I had the pleasure of feeling his lips on my cheek, ears, and neck. But I hadn't felt them on mine yet. Putting both hands on either side of my face, he leaned in and softly kissed my lips.

"For this week, you're mine. I have to be honest with you, though. I'm not really looking for a relationship right now, especially not a long distance one," he said.

I hadn't thought beyond this week, so his confession was cool with me. If he let me ride his dick every night for the next seven days, I'd be satisfied. The dick print in the khakis he wore told me that I'd be more than satisfied.

"I think we're on the same page, Mr. Ross."

This time, when his lips landed on mine, our tongues also intertwined. The flavor of the liquor he drank earlier mixed with mine as we devoured each other. He lifted my dress and we parted briefly so that he could lift it over my head. Tossing it to the side, he took a step back, allowing his eyes to travel up and down the length of my body.

I had already taken off my shoes and I wasn't wearing a bra, so I stood there in a pair of black lace panties. Before he touched me again, he undressed himself, leaving only his boxer briefs on. Now it was my turn to admire his body and damn, it was a sight to see.

My hand went to his firm chest and he grabbed my wrist and pulled my body against his. As his lips caressed the length of my neck and found their way to my breast, I thought about how long it had been since a man had touched me this way. Closing my eyes, I got lost in the moment.

Suddenly, my panties ripped and he lifted my legs around his waist. My center rubbing against his thickness felt good enough for me to cum. He walked us to the bed, where he fell on top of me. My hands went to push his underwear down, and with his help, soon we were both naked. I had to take a deep breath when I saw the size of his dick. My ass got nervous, like I was a virgin.

He moved away from the bed, dick standing at attention, and went to his suitcase. When he returned, he had on a condom, and tossed two more on the nightstand. Turning off the lamp, he crawled to meet me at the center of the bed and positioned his body over mine.

"I don't think I've ever seen a woman so beautiful. You fine as fuck."

I smiled at his compliment. "I'm about to give you all of this pussy. You don't have to compliment me."

"But it's true. If your pussy feels as good as you look, my ass might be in trouble."

He placed himself between my legs and we kissed like two teenagers in an intense make-out session. The friction of us grinding against each other brought me to a climax so quick that I was almost embarrassed. But it felt too good for me to care.

I pulled my mouth away from his and said, "Shit, Kolby, I'm about to cum."

"Let that shit go, baby girl."

Then his ass had the nerve to push his thick, long, slightly curved dick into my haven, right as I was exploding and *damn*, that shit felt so fucking good.

Kolby Ross

I ENTERED her swiftly but stroked her slowly and deeply. "Got damn, Myla. You tight as fuck."

I've had my share of pussy, but it's been a long-ass time since I've had some pussy this tight. My ass might have to bust one and wait until round two to really put in work.

"Ahh, shit," she moaned.

Her legs tightened around my waist, urging me to go deeper. I told her I wasn't looking for a relationship but this pussy got me thinking I spoke too damn soon. I already didn't want to think of her giving this good ass pussy to another nigga.

"Shit!" I groaned. "I'm in trouble."

"Oh my Gaa, I'm cummin'," she mumbled into my neck.

During the planning of this trip, I didn't anticipate that I would be knee-deep in Myla's pussy. She had a real cool vibe about her and I thought it was dope that her and Jaelynn wanted to reconnect Braelynn and Kyree. Over the past several months, we'd only communicated as a group.

When I saw her in person, her beauty took my breath away. I'd looked through her Instagram a while back but it mostly had pictures from their lingerie company. Today, it was like I was seeing her for the first time. Her chocolate skin was so smooth and flawless. Her lips were plump and perfectly shaped. Her dimpled left cheek was sexy as hell. Her natural hair was thick and long enough for me to grip. I'm not gonna even start on her body.

"Baby girl, why you so fuckin' tight? I'm about to bust," I warned.

My strokes became faster but remained deep. I felt her pussy contract around my dick, letting me know that she was about to reach her peak again. When we exploded together, I thought that I had died and gone to heaven. Breathless and seeing stars, I pulled out of her and fell to the side, then wrapped her in my arms.

All that could be heard was our breathing for a few minutes. My hand rubbed up and down her arm as hers did the same to my chest. Finally, she spoke.

"I have a confession."

"Please don't tell me you were a virgin."

Her pussy was so tight that I began to wonder.

She laughed. "No, I'm not a virgin but...I haven't had sex in three years."

"Three years? Shit, you may as well be a virgin. Why didn't you tell me that beforehand?"

"Because I didn't want you to change your mind. I was really horny and I think I would have died if you had denied me the dick."

It was my turn to laugh. "I wouldn't have denied you but I would have been a little gentler. Did I hurt you?"

I kissed her forehead and held my breath as I waited for her to answer.

"Not at all. She was nice and wet for you because I came as you entered me."

"Good. I still wish you would have said something. I knew you were unusually tight."

"I'm also unusually horny. Once these seven days are up, I'll probably be on another three-year drought. Let's do it again."

I cracked up at her ass sounding like a horny teenager.

"Shit, you ain't gotta ask twice."

Over the next seven days, Myla and I spent quite a bit of time together, getting to know each other. I learned more about her in a week than I did about most of the women that I dated. I ended up moving my shit into the room with Myla and we sexed every night like it was our last. Thankfully, Kamden and Jaelynn didn't mind.

By the time our last day arrived, I had grown pretty attached to her. I kept my feelings to myself since I was the one that brought up not wanting to be in a relationship. After spending the week with her, if she had brought it up to me, I would have definitely given it a shot.

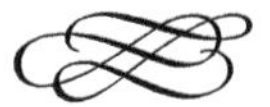

Three Months Later

Kolby

Flying to Seattle with Kyree wasn't in my plans but when he mentioned catching a lastminute flight, Kamden suggested we roll with him for moral support. I only agreed because I had another reason for going, but I decided to keep it to myself.

My brother had gotten himself in some deep shit with his ex-girlfriend, Leah, and was headed to Seattle to break up with his new girl, Braelynn. Kamden and I didn't think a break-up was necessary, but he didn't want Braelynn involved in all the drama that he knew Leah would cause.

When we arrived in Seattle, we picked up the truck that Kyree rented for our short visit and drove to our destination. Jaelynn opened the door and was understandably surprised to see us.

"Is she here?" Kyree asked.

Without saying anything, she stepped to the side, giving us room to enter.

"Umm, Brae. Can you come here for a second?" Jaelynn called out.

"You don't see my purse?" Braelynn yelled from somewhere in the house.

She came into the living room and right behind her was Myla. *Damn!* I wasn't expecting to see her right at that moment. She was more beautiful than I remembered. Over the past three months, we've texted a few times but not as much as I would have liked. I thought about her and the time we spent in Belize, every day.

I could see by her expression that she was surprised to see me, as well. When her hand went to her stomach, my eyes followed, and unless they were deceiving me, she looked...pregnant. I tried to connect my eyes with hers, but they avoided mine.

When Kyree and Braelynn went to her room, Jaelynn pulled Kamden into the kitchen. Myla hadn't moved and it was clear that she didn't plan on it. I went and stood in front of her, close enough to touch her if I wanted to. My hands were in my pockets, as I waited for her to say something and when she didn't, I did.

"Hi."

"Hi."

"How have you, umm, been?"

Without warning, she burst out in tears. My hands came out of my pockets and I pulled her into my arms. I knew why she was crying, but I wanted her to tell me.

"Myla, baby, what's wrong?"

She didn't answer me right away because she was crying too hard. After a few minutes of us standing there, while she cried into my chest, she lifted her head. Her eyes were red and still watery but her tears had slowed.

"I'm sorry."

"Sorry about what?"

"Kolby, I'm pregnant and the baby is yours."

My hands went to her little bump. "Why didn't you tell me?"

"I wanted to...so many times, but I didn't know how you would react."

We could hear the voices of Kyree and Braelynn going back and forth with each other.

"Is there somewhere we can go and talk? Our flight back, isn't until tomorrow."

"We can go to my place."

"Okay. Let me tell Kam and grab my bag out of the truck."

When I went in the kitchen, Kamden and Jaelynn were sitting at the table, in what looked to be a deep conversation. Jaelynn had her arms folded across her chest, defensively.

"Aye, I'm gonna stay with Myla tonight. We're about to leave."

"She good?" Kamden asked.

"She's pregnant."

"Oh, shit."

"Yeah."

"So, how you feeling about that?" he asked.

"I hate I had to find out like this but I'm good. I'll hit you up in the morning. Unlock the truck."

In the living room, Myla had her jacket on and was standing by the door. My eyes roamed her body and I had flashbacks of how our bodies became one, night after night, while we were in Belize.

"Are you ready?" she asked, pulling me from my thoughts.

"Oh, yeah."

When we got outside, she went to her car while I got my bag from the truck. I hopped in the passenger side, and we were on our way. The whole ride to her place, we didn't speak. I had questions, but didn't want her to get emotional while driving.

About fifteen minutes later, she pulled into her driveway and turned the car off.

"Why don't you park in the garage?" I asked.

"It's small and I have a lot of my brother's stuff in there. Makes me feel claustrophobic."

Nodding, I got out and grabbed my bag out of the back seat. When I looked up, she was on the walkway waiting for me.

"Why didn't you wait for me to open your door?" I asked.

She frowned. "Because I can open it myself."

We walked to the front door of her house and when she went to put her key in the door, I took the keys away from her.

"When we're together, I'll open all doors. Which key is it?"

She pointed to the key and I unlocked the door, pushing it open. After allowing her to enter, I followed and locked the door behind us. Putting my bag on the floor by the door, I took my shoes off and put them next to Myla's. I found her in the kitchen looking in the fridge.

"Shit, girl!" I said when I saw her bent over inside the fridge. It reminded me of when we were in Belize and I responded the same way to her doing the same thing.

"Shut up! Probably all fat and outta shape, now that I'm pregnant. Do you want some water or something?"

"I'm good. And your ass is not fat and outta shape. You look beautiful carrying my seed."

Her eyes met mine and she gave me a slight smile.

"You're not gonna question whether or not it's yours?"

I frowned. "Let's go sit down and talk."

She led me into her living room and we sat next to each other on the couch.

"Why would I question whether or not this is my seed?"

"Isn't that what most men would do in this situation?"

"I'm not most men. Is that why you were afraid to tell me?"

"Mostly."

"Why else were you afraid?"

"You made it clear that you weren't interested in a long-term or long distance, one-on-one relationship. Me getting pregnant just seemed...I don't know...kind of suspect."

"Suspect? If that's the case, we both exhibited some suspect behavior that week. I'm well aware that not one, but two condoms broke. And let's not forget our last night together. We didn't use anything at all that night, Myla. Honestly, we both knew this was a strong possibility."

She nodded. "I guess we both have to take responsibility for how this happened."

"What matters most right now, is that we both want this baby. I'll be with you every step of the way. I would never let you go through this alone."

She stood and began pacing back and forth. I could tell that her mind was going a mile a minute.

"How Kolby? You live in Chicago."

I grabbed her hand to stop her from pacing.

"Sit down, please. You need to calm down, baby."

She sat back down next to me and I took her hands in mine.

"When is your next appointment?" I asked.

"Not for another month. I went a couple of days ago to see how far along I was and I heard the heartbeat."

"Wow."

She left me there briefly and returned with her purse. Digging inside, she retrieved an envelope and gave it to me. When I opened it and pulled out the ultrasound, a nigga got teary-eyed.

"This is our baby?"

"It is. The heartbeat was really strong. I'm sorry I didn't tell you as soon as I found out. I just—"

"Don't worry about it. I know now and that's all that matters."

I continued looking at the ultrasound, completely in awe that I had created another human being.

"Is he moving yet?"

She looked at me with a strange expression. "You said 'he'. How do you know it's a boy?"

"Did I?" I shrugged my shoulders. "I don't know because I really don't have a preference. I just want our baby to be healthy."

She smiled for the first time since I laid eyes on her today. "I haven't felt any movement yet. From what I read, maybe in a few more weeks."

"I'll be here for the rest of our appointments. I don't want to miss any of them."

"You don't—"

"Don't even say that shit, My. I know this ain't what we planned, but let me be here for you as much as I can. We'll figure everything else out as we go."

"Okay."

As reckless as we were in Belize, I hadn't thought much about the possibility of Myla getting pregnant. Being a father at this point in my life wasn't on my radar but for some reason, I feel like this was meant to be.

MYLA

The last person I expected to see today was Kolby. He looked so damn good, too. I was so nervous about how he would take the news about me carrying his child but it went a lot better than I expected. He seemed to be excited about becoming a father.

Once we finished our discussion about the baby, we ordered a pizza and watched reruns of *The Cosby Show*. This baby had already started to zap my energy and I yawned. When I readjusted myself on the couch, Kolby pulled my feet onto his lap and rubbed them with a firm hand. If he wanted me to stay awake, this certainly wouldn't help.

I heard myself moan and felt his dick jump underneath my feet. My head popped up and our eyes connected.

"You can't be moaning like that, My."

"I'm sorry. It just feels so good."

"Why don't I go take a shower so you can go to bed?"

"You're staying the night, right?"

"That's why I got my bag, baby. I haven't seen you in three months. I planned to changed that before I knew about the baby."

I smiled at the thought of him wanting to spend time with me.

"I'll probably fall asleep in the tub. Your child has had me exhausted."

He turned off the T.V. and moved my feet from his lap. His dick print was still on display in the navy-blue sweats he was wearing. I tore my eyes away from it and went to my bedroom, while he went to get his bag from near the door.

"Can you turn the alarm on? The code is zero-nine-two-four."

I heard him turning on the alarm as I walked into my master bathroom . By the time I started the shower and walked back into my room, Kolby had put his bag on the floor and was sitting on the bench in front of my queen-sized bed.

I wasn't sure what would happen between us and I didn't have any expectations. He didn't say that his stance on being in a relationship had changed and honestly, I didn't want him to change it just because I was pregnant. What I did know, was that I was horny and he was the only person I wanted. I couldn't count the number of wet dreams I'd had about him since Belize.

On my way to my drawer to grab a T-shirt to sleep in, he pulled me into his arms. When I looked up at him, his head was bent toward mine and our lips were only an inch apart.

"Can I kiss you?"

"Ye—"

His lips were on my before I could say yes. My arms went around his neck and I pressed my body against his. I opened my mouth to receive his tongue and it battled to control the flow of the kiss. I didn't care who had control, as long as he didn't stop kissing me. I was so caught up in the goodness of his lips on mine, that I literally forgot to breathe. Suddenly, I pulled away and took a step back.

"Shit, My. I'm sorry for getting carried away. I just missed you so fucking much."

Still breathing hard, I said, "You missed me?"

"Every day."

"Oh."

I had to let that ponder for a bit.

"Can I shower with you?"

Hell yeah!

"We better hurry before the water gets cold."

"I'm sure it needs to cool off, anyway," he teased because like most women, I liked my water nice and hot.

As I expected, the bathroom was full of steam, but when we stripped down, that steam couldn't hide his dick standing at attention. When my eyes landed on it, I think my pussy did a lil' twerk. She remembered how good his dick was to her and wanted another dose.

"Kolby, have you had sex with anyone since Belize?"

"Since I had you, I haven't wanted to be with anybody else."

I found that hard to believe but he had no reason to lie. I got in the shower first, and he came in right behind me. He put his arms around me from behind and rested his hands on my stomach. I leaned my head back and to the side, giving his mouth access to my cheek, then my earlobe, then he moved down to my neck. His hands cupped my breasts, which were a bit fuller and definitely more sensitive than ever.

He turned me around and pressed me against the wall. With his forehead against mine, he said, "I really did miss you."

I grabbed the sides of his face and kissed him, with more passion than I had ever kissed another man. When his hands went to the underside of my ass and he lifted me, my legs clamped around his waist. My hand went between us and I placed him at my entrance. He pushed inside of me and pulled his mouth away from mine and said, "Damn, I've missed you!"

Then he began to stroke me nice, slow, and deep. Oh my God, I wanted to cry. I wanted to literally shed tears. I don't know if it was my hormones, or if it was because I'd been dreaming about having his dick inside me again for the last three months. I had heard that sex was better when you're pregnant, maybe it was that. All I knew was my ass was in heaven.

"Shit, My, you feel so fucking good."

His knees lowered, allowing him to go deeper. With my head pressed against the shower wall, I turned it from left to right because I didn't know what else to do. This couldn't feel this good and I began to think it was another wet dream. His mouth went to my nipples and it took me to the edge. My pussy began to contract around his big-ass dick, milking him of his seeds.

"Shit, baby, I'm about to cum," I screamed.

Our eyes connected and his glare was too strong, so I closed mine.

"Look at me, baby. Look at me while you cream all over this dick."

"Ahhh," I moaned as I looked in his eyes.

"Fuck," he grunted as he looked back at me.

The tempo of his strokes sped up, then slowed down gradually. He rested his head on my shoulder and mine rested on his chest. The water began to cool, causing us to disconnect our union and quickly bathe ourselves.

Thirty minutes later, Kolby was in my bed, naked, already asleep. Since my hair had gotten wet in the shower, I had to braid it up so it wouldn't be matted to my head in the morning. After turning off all the lights, I climbed into bed next to him. His arms went around my waist and he rested his hand on my stomach.

"Why are you wearing this?" he asked.

"I usually sleep in a T-shirt."

"Not when I'm here. Take it off."

He helped me out by pushing it up and I sat up and took it the rest of the way off.

"That's better. Goodnight." He kissed my shoulder.

"Goodnight."

Lying in his arms felt good, I wished I could do it every night. Unfortunately, our circumstances didn't allow that and I'm not even sure that it was something he wanted.

KOLBY

The next morning, I woke up to an empty bed and the smell of bacon. After emptying my bladder, washing my hands and face, then brushing my teeth, I pulled on a pair basketball shorts and went to the kitchen. Myla was standing at the stove with her back facing me, so I snuck up behind her and put my hands around her waist.

"Shit! Kolby, you scared me."

I moved her away from the oven and leaned her against the counter. After kissing her a few times, I apologized.

"I'm sorry, baby. What are you cooking?"

"I remembered that you like spinach and cheese omelets, so I made one for you, with some bacon on the side."

"Thank you, My. I appreciate it. Our flight is at three. What are your plans today?" I picked up a piece of bacon and took a bite.

"Well, I was wondering if you would mind meeting my mother and brother?"

"That's cool. What time?"

"Are you sure?"

"Yeah, I'm sure. What time?"

"Whenever we get ready. They don't know you're in town, but they both expressed that they wanted to meet you when I told them I was pregnant."

"That's understandable. What about your father?"

"What about him? I haven't seen him since I was in elementary school."

"That's unfortunate." She shrugged her shoulders.

I walked my plate of food to the other side of the breakfast bar and sat on one of the stools. Myla brought me a glass of orange juice and sat next to me.

"Did you eat already?" I asked when I noticed she didn't have a plate.

"I'm not really hungry. I had a couple of pieces of toast while I cooked for you."

I frowned at her because I didn't think two pieces of toast was enough for someone with a child growing inside of her.

"That's it? You know you're eating for two now, right?""My appetite has been up and down and I still feel nauseous sometimes."

"I'm sorry, My. You've been going through all this by yourself."

"Why are you apologizing? You didn't even know."

"I still feel bad. I hate that I have to leave you today. You have to promise to FaceTime me every day, multiple times a day, and put the phone up to your stomach so I can talk to the baby."

"Whatever you want, I'll do it."

"Okay. Eat some of this omelet."

I put some on my fork and lifted it to her mouth. I could tell she didn't want to but she did anyway. I ended up feeding her half of it.

"Why don't you go shower and I'll—"

Her hand suddenly went to cover her mouth and she ran to the powder room. I didn't know what the fuck was going on so I ran after her. She made it to the toilet in just enough time to empty her insides.

"Oh shit!"

I kneeled down next to her and rubbed her back until she finished. She lifted her head from the toilet and sat on the floor, leaning her back against the wall.

"I'm gonna go get you some water. Where is your linen closet?"

"In the hall," she whispered with her head between her legs.

I went to grab a towel out of her linen closet and then back to the kitchen to get a bottle of water. When I got back to the bathroom, her head was against the wall and her eyes were closed.

"Take a few sips of this," I said, opening the bottle for her.

While she sipped the water, I wet the face towel with cool water. Kneeling down next to her, I dabbed her forehead with the towel.

"You okay?"

She nodded.

"I'm so fuckin' sorry, My. Has it been bad?"

Shrugging her shoulders, she said, "I don't have anything to compare it to. I mean, it's been manageable."

"You feel okay enough to stand up?"

"Yeah."

I helped her up, and we slowly walked to her bedroom. She sat on her bed and I kneeled in front of her.

"Kolby, my breath is probably humming right now. Get away."

She gently pushed me away and tried to scoot back on the bed.

"I don't give a shit about your breath. I'm trying to make sure you're okay. It's my fault you're feeling like this, anyway."

"It's nobody's fault. We're both extra-grown and things happen."

"Yeah, okay. I'm gonna go clean up the kitchen while you relax. I'll be back in a few."

She nodded and fell back on the bed. I hated seeing her like this but there wasn't much I could do now. It only took me about ten minutes to clean up the kitchen. When I went back to her bedroom, Myla had fallen asleep. Instead of waking her, I showered and got dressed.

She was still asleep, and as much as I hated to wake her, if she still wanted me to meet her family, we needed to be leaving soon.

"Baby, wake up."

She opened her eyes and covered her mouth as she yawned.

"Shit! What time is it?"

"Eleven. We still have time. Do you need help with your shower?"

She frowned and shook her head. "Kolby, I'm not handicapped, just pregnant. I do this every day without help."

The attitude in her voice shocked me. Instead of replying, I let her do her thing.

"I'll be in the living room watching T.V. when you're ready."

Grabbing my duffle bag, I left her in the bedroom. Thirty minutes later, she stood in front of me, where I was sitting on the couch, wearing a pair of black Nike leggings and a Nike zip up hoodie. It looked like she only had on a sports bra underneath.

"You ready?"

"Whenever you are, Myla."

When I stood, we were close enough to touch. She wrapped her arms around my neck and kissed my lips.

"I want to apologize for my attitude. I can be a little moody at times."

I kissed her before replying. "It's cool. Let's go. I'm supposed to meet my brothers at the airport at one-thirty."

MYLA

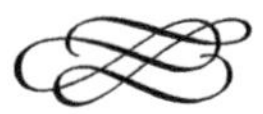

When we arrived at my mom's house, I saw my brother's car in the driveway. I'd sent him a text and told him to make sure he was there if he wanted to meet the father of my child. My mom was home in the middle of the day because she had taken a couple of days off to attend the funeral of one of her high school classmates. I parked behind my brother's car and looked at Kolby.

"I haven't told them much about you. They do know that we met in Belize and that you're Braelynn's boyfriend's brother, but that's about it."

"That's cool. They can ask me whatever they want to know."

"My brother is a hood nigga so don't pay him no mind."

"Myla, don't worry so much."

He got out and came around to open my door. We held hands as we approached the door. I used my key to let us inside. Kolby looked at me and I believe the only reason he didn't say something about me opening the door was because it was my mom's house.

"Where y'all at?" I asked once we were inside.

"In the family room," Mommy responded.

I took my Nike running shoes off and Kolby did the same with his shoes. He followed me into the family room, where we found my brother sitting in the recliner and my mom sitting on the couch.

"Hey guys. This is Kolby."

He approached my mother to greet her. She stood when he took her hand, looking at him with googly eyes.

"It's a pleasure to meet you Ms. Gentry," Kolby said, before placing a kiss on her hand.

"Please, call me Dalilah."

"Okay, *Ms.* Dalilah."

I'd already told him my mother's last name, so that he would assume that ours were the same.

Without getting up, Myles gave Kolby the once-over as he approached. Kolby put his hand out for a shake.

"This is my, 'no-manners-having,' older brother, Myles."

"Wassup?" Kolby said.

Myles returned the handshake and said, "So, you the nigga that knocked up my baby sis?"

"Myles! Oh my God!"

I sat on the loveseat and put my face in my hands. Embarrassed wasn't a strong enough word to describe how I felt. When I felt the cushion sink next to me, I looked up and saw Kolby.

"I *am* the nigga that knocked up your baby sis. Is that a problem?"

"Not if you gon' take care of her and my niece or nephew," Myles replied.

"Mommy, get him please."

"Myles, could be a bit more polite; but honestly, I would like to know how you two are gonna work this out."

"If you're wondering if I plan to support her and the baby financially, yes, I do."

"Ain't you from Chicago? You plan on moving here?" Myles just wouldn't let up.

"Myles, I told y'all that we weren't in a relationship. This just kinda happened. I don't expect him to move here."

"Sis, I was asking him."

"I just found out she was pregnant last night. We haven't really discussed the logistics of everything. Just know that she's not in this alone and I'll be here in whatever way she needs me."

Myles and my mom looked at us for a good minute. I felt like a damn teenager with the way they were glaring at us.

"I guess we'll have to see how this shit work out. You cool with me until Myla tells me you fuckin' up."

"Myles, watch your mouth. I swear your ass is so disrespectful," Mommy said.

Myles was as hood as they come. He's been selling drugs since high school, and has never had a regular job. I guess he makes good money because he's never asked us for anything and is very generous with us. Lately, he's been trying to go legit, which is why he moved back in with my mom and got all his shit in my garage. He ain't really shared his plans, and I don't get involved in his shit, so I haven't asked him.

"My bad, Ma. You know how I am with My. That's my baby and she's having a baby." He looked at Kolby. "My bad, homie. I wasn't trying to be disrespectful, this just who I am."

"It's cool."

For the next twenty minutes or so, my mom asked Kolby questions about his family and his job as an accountant. When she asked if he would be able to make it to my appointments, he assured her that he planned to be at every one of them. We left shortly thereafter, stopping to have *Dick's Drive-In* for lunch on the way to the airport.

"I wish I could stay longer," he said.

"I'll be fine. You'll be back in a month for my appointment, right?"

"I told you, your mother, and your brother that I would. I'm a man of my word, Myla. You can trust what I say."

"Okay."

Dick's had the best burgers in town, but I could only eat half of mine. When Kolby noticed me wrapping the other half up, he frowned.

"Baby, you gotta eat more. Is this normal?"

"It is. I can't eat a lot at once because I get sick. I make sure I drink a lot of water and I eat healthy snacks. Don't worry, your baby is not starving."

"I need to do some research, because I don't know shit about pregnancy."

"Me either. I've been reading articles on the internet. I'm sure there are some books I could get, too."

I looked at the time and realized we needed to get going. Securing my seatbelt, I pulled out of the drive-in and drove him to the airport. When we arrived, I parked by the curb. He leaned across the console and planted a kiss on my lips.

"We got this, okay. We'll be good," he assured me.

I nodded in agreement. "Text me when you get home and let me know you made it."

"I'll FaceTime you so I can talk to the baby, too."

I laughed. "Okay."

We kissed again before he got out. Once he retrieved his bag from the back seat, I left.

On my way home, my phone rang. I saw Braelynn's name on the display and answered through my car's Bluetooth.

"Hey, Brae! Is everything cool with you and Kyree?"

"Yeah, it's fine. The nigga tried to break up with me because his ex-girlfriend is pregnant."

"Wow! Really? He didn't cheat, did he?"

"No. She was pregnant before they broke up. For the last few days, he's been trying to get her to agree to a DNA test but she refuses. He doesn't think it's his, but they were fucking so there's a possibility."

"There sure is. Even if he wrapped up. Damn! I hate that for y'all, but I'm glad everything is good."

"Me too. What about you and Kolby? How did he take the news?"

"Honestly, really well. I think he was hurt that I didn't tell him right away, but he wasn't upset."

"I told your ass you were worrying for nothing. Ms. Stella and Mr. Isaac raised some great men. She's gonna be so excited when she finds out that Kolby is having a baby."

"You don't think she's excited about Kyree's baby?"

She laughed. "I haven't talked to her about it yet but I have a feeling it's going to be a colorful conversation. She can't stand his ex."

"Uh oh. Should I be worried?"

"Naw. Ms. Stella gon' love you. Once Kolby tells her the situation, she'll be cool."

"I hope so. Well, I'm home now. I haven't done anything boutique-related today and I know I'm gonna regret it tomorrow. I just wanna take a nap."

"Me and Jae got it for the rest of the day. Get some rest. I know Kolby had you up all night tappin' that ass," Braelynn teased.

"Mind your business, heffa. Bye."

I ended the call before she said anything else. I would have been crazy to let Kolby leave town without getting some dick. Hell, I'm already pregnant by the nigga. When I got home, I finished the other half of the burger from Dick's and took a nap.

Some time later, I was awakened by my phone. My room was dark, so I must have been asleep for a while.

"Hello," I answered without seeing who is was.

"Hey, baby. Did I wake you?" It was Kolby.

"Yeah."

"You must be tired. I tried to FaceTime you, too."

"Really?" I said before yawning. "I didn't hear my phone. I'll FaceTime you back in a few minutes. Let me go use the bathroom."

"Okay."

I didn't move for a few minutes after the call ended. If this baby had me this tired now, I couldn't imagine what it would be like in a few months. I got up and used the bathroom. While I washed my hands, I looked in the mirror and decided to put my hair in two braids before calling him back. Once I did that, I got undressed. I was about to put on one of the many T-shirts that I slept in, but I spotted the T-shirt that Kolby had on yesterday and put that on instead. I got comfortable in my bed, and FaceTimed him.

"Hey. How you feeling?" he answered.

"I'm good. I'll probably go back to bed when we hang up, though."

"Did you eat?"

"Before I took my nap, I finished the rest of my burger. I've been sleeping since then."

"So, that would be a no."

"I guess so. I'll eat before I go back to sleep. How was your flight?"

"It was fine. I want you to eat something while we're on the phone, My."

I rolled my eyes and exhaled. "Fine."

I got out of bed and put my slides on, then went to the kitchen and looked in the fridge. All I saw that I wanted were pineapples and strawberries. As I made myself a bowl, we didn't speak. When I sat at the breakfast bar, I pointed the phone towards my bowl of fruit.

"You happy now?"

"I am. Did you talk to your mother and brother after our visit?"

"No, but I talked to Braelynn. Sounds like you *and* your brother are about to become fathers."

"Yeah. He's praying that the baby ain't his, though. I'm glad you're having my baby."

"Really? Why?"

"I think you're a great person and I think you'll be an even greater mother."

"Aww, thank you, Kolby. I think you'll be a great father, too. Have you told your parents?"

"Not yet. I'll probably stop by there and tell them tomorrow. They'll be cool about it."

"You think so?"

"Yeah. My mom will want to meet you right away, and he'll be disappointed that you don't live closer; but you don't have anything to worry about."

"I hope not."

I finished up the fruit while he stared at me through the phone. It made absolutely no sense for him to be as fine as he was. His gaze was making me hot through the damn phone.

"Okay, I'm done with my fruit. I'm about to brush my teeth and go back to bed. I didn't do any work today, and I got a lot of catching up to do tomorrow."

"That's cool. Let me talk to my baby first."

I washed my bowl and fork, then grabbed a bottle of water out of the fridge. In my bedroom, I put the water bottle on my nightstand and went to the bathroom, where the lights were nice and bright. Lifting up my shirt, I put the phone up to my stomach.

"Hey, Baby Ross. This is your daddy. I want you to get used to my voice, so I'm gonna be talking to you a lot. I'm already excited to meet you. Make sure you don't give your mommy a hard time. Daddy's not there to help her, so you gotta be on your best behavior. I love you already and I'll talk to you tomorrow."

I didn't realize that I was crying until a tear dripped on the phone. Never would I have imagined him being such a sweetheart. I feel so stupid about not telling him I was pregnant right away.

"Hold on a sec," I told him.

After washing my face, I picked up the phone and looked into his handsome face.

"You good?"

"Yeah. I'm good."

I was still standing in the bathroom because I wanted to brush my teeth when we hung up.

"Are you crying? What's wrong?"

I thought I had gotten myself together but there were some tears lingering.

"Nothing bad. You're just really sweet, and I'm super emotional. That's all."

"I didn't mean to make you cry, baby. I was simply speaking from my heart."

"I know. I'm gonna brush my teeth and go back to bed. I guess you can call me tomorrow. Or I'll call you. Or...whatever."

Ignoring me, he said, "Is that my T-shirt?"

I looked down at his T-shirt that I'd forgotten I was wearing. "It *was*, but you left it here. It's mine now."

He laughed. "Oh, it's like that?"

"Just like that. Goodnight!"

I ended the call and put my phone on the counter. It vibrated while I brushed my teeth but I didn't look at it until I was done.

KR: I kinda like the idea of you sleeping in my shirt. I'll make sure I leave a few every time I visit.

Me: Works for me. Goodnight.

KR: Goodnight.

KOLBY

It had been two weeks since I found out I was going to be a father. When I told my parents, my mother wanted to know everything there was to know about Myla. They ended up talking on FaceTime and I had to reiterate to my mother before I called that we were not in a relationship. Not that it mattered to her. Stella was gon' say what Stella wanted to say, regardless. I had to take the phone away from her because she was doing too damn much.

She forced me to give her Myla's number so she could check on her and get to know her. I didn't want to, but she threatened my life and Stella don't play. My dad was cool about it, but he sat me down and asked me what my plans were with her. I shook my head as I thought back to that conversation.

"Your brother already has a baby on the way with a woman that he has no intention on being with. I know he says it's not his, but we don't know that right now. Do you and this young lady plan to co-parent while living in different cities?"

"Man, Dad, I don't have the answer to that right now."

"Why not, son? This is your baby, correct?"

"It is. I'm a hundred sure about that."

"Then you need to figure it out. The baby will be here before you know it. Do you have feelings for her?"

He was sitting in his recliner and I was on the couch, sitting on the end closest to him. In my head and heart, that was an easy answer. Yes, I have feelings for Myla. But to say those words aloud...

"Son, why is that a hard question to answer?" he continued when I didn't answer.

"Because when we hooked up in Belize, I was so sure about not wanting to be in a relationship. I made sure I told her before anything went down, that I wasn't looking for a relationship and definitely not a long distance one."

"And?"

"And she was cool with it. She said we were on the same page. The more time we spent together, the more I regretted telling her that. I could tell that she was feeling me too, but she didn't bring it up again and neither did I."

"Do you want a relationship now?"

Again, I didn't answer right away and my dad was getting frustrated.

"What the hell is wrong with you, boy? If you want to be with the girl, tell her. She's probably waiting for you to make the first move since you're the one that made a point to take a relationship off the table."

"I don't know, Dad. I don't want her to think I want a relationship now just because she's pregnant."

"Well, considering the circumstances, she may very well think that. It's your job to make sure she knows otherwise."

The night that Myla told me that she was pregnant, as she slept soundly, it took me a while to settle into a good sleep because I couldn't turn my brain off. I thought back to our time in Belize. We had sex every night and the condom broke twice. She didn't seem overly concerned about it, neither was I. But, I'm almost sure she got pregnant on our last night together.

I went into the bathroom while she showered. My intent was to get my toiletries together so I wouldn't have to worry about it in the morning. However, when I saw her naked body, I lost all control.

I took off my shorts and opened the glass door. She was startled but when she saw me, she smiled.

"Get in and close the door. You're letting in all the cold air."

I stepped in and closed the door. "Woman, you got this damn shower set on hell. You don't feel shit but heat."

I penned her against the wall and covered her mouth with mine. Our tongues intertwined immediately and we French kissed for a good five minutes. My dick was hard, pressed between our stomachs. She put her arms around my neck and I felt one of her legs trying to go around my waist. When I realized what she was trying to do, I lifted her by the ass and reached between us, shoving my dick into her wet hole.

"Ahh, shit!" she mumbled against my chest.

It was then that I realized that I wasn't wearing a condom. I could have nutted right then and there. Her pussy felt so good. It was warm, wet, and so damn snug. My knees got weak with the first stroke. I prayed that she would cum quickly because I knew I would. And I promised myself that I would pull out.

My dick must have been just as good to Myla. From her position against the wall, with her legs around my waist, she was trying to match my strokes. I didn't have as much control over the situation as I thought I did, and before I could process it all, we came simultaneously. And that was all she wrote.

Neither of us brought up the fact that I wasn't wearing a condom and later that night when we had sex again and again, I couldn't imagine having a barrier between us. So, as I told her, her getting pregnant shouldn't have been a surprise to either of us.

If Myla would have me, I'd be her man in a heartbeat, but I would hate for her to think that I'm only with her because she's carrying my seed. We'd been communicating every day, all day, through FaceTime and text; we've talked about everything but us. I decided to wait until I went out there in a couple of weeks for her doctor's appointment to bring it up.

My phone rang, pulling me out of my thoughts. I was surprised to see Corette's name on my screen. She was a flight attendant and someone I fucked around with from time to time. She was from Atlanta and had been only doing international flights for the past three months. We talked or texted occasionally, but not recently.

"Hey," I answered.

"What's up, K?"

"Nothing much. What's up with you?"

"Same shit, different day. I'm actually in Toronto and since it's only an hour ahead, I figured I'd give you a call. I miss you."

"Really? Are you sure it's me you miss? Or is it this dick?"

She giggled. "Both. I'll be in Chicago next month. We should hook up."

"You still on a nigga. Those international niggas ain't keeping you occupied?"

"Not like Kolby."

"Yeah, okay."

"I'll hit you up when I know an exact date. Nothing's set in stone right now."

"Cool."

"Bye, K."

"Bye."

Corette was cool people and we had fun together. All we did was have sex, maybe grab a meal somewhere, but most of the time we ordered in from her hotel room. Our little situationship had been going on for a couple of years. Since I wasn't involved with anyone on a serious level, I never had a reason to end it. Maybe it was time, though.

MYLA

I could hardly contain my excitement. My four-month prenatal appointment was in a couple of days, and Kolby was flying in tonight. Not only do I get to see him, we may also get to find out the sex of the baby. We both decided that we wanted to know the sex right away, and neither of us were interested in having a gender reveal party.

Since I was feeling good, I decided to make veggie burrito bowls. As I cut up the vegetables, I got a call from Jaelynn saying her and Braelynn were going to stop by if I was up for company. I'm always down to hang with my girls so I told them to come on over. When they arrived, they updated me on the drama between Kyree and Braelynn. He seemed like such a good guy but what they told me sounded real suspect. I couldn't even defend him.

Once that discussion was over, we discussed our lingerie business. We'd been trying to lease a building for months, but every time we found one, something happened that caused us not to get the building. They had just found out that Braelynn's ex, Samuel, was behind at least one that we'd lost out on. I couldn't stand

Samuel's bitch-ass. We continued to brainstorm when we finished eating, and just as they were about to leave, my doorbell rang.

"Uh oh, your boo is here," Braelynn teased.

"Stop, Brae! You know we aren't together."

I opened the door without looking through the peephole, and Kolby stepped inside and immediately started fussing at me.

"Do you always answer the door without checking to see who it is?"

"I'm not expecting anyone but you."

He pulled me into his arms for a hug, and when he released me, his hands went right to my stomach.

"You still need to check. Too many crazy people out there, and you got precious cargo in here. How's my baby treating you today?"

"Today's been good, so far."

"Oh, hey, Jae, Brae. I didn't see y'all over here. Wassup?" Kolby greeted them.

"That's because you only got eyes for my girl," Jaelynn teased.

He looked at me and winked, causing me to smile.

"We were just leaving. My, I'll check on you tomorrow," Braelynn said as they moved toward the door.

We all exchanged hugs as they made their exit. However, Jaelynn couldn't leave without saying something about Kyree.

"Tell Kyree that was some fuck shit he let ole girl do last night."

Kolby was clearly unaware of what Jaelynn was referring to, based on the confused look on his face.

"What are you talking about? Who is *ole girl*?"

"Jae, let's just go. This isn't Kolby's problem," Braelynn said.

"No, wait," Kolby touched Braelynn's arm. "What happened?"

"He let that hoe send pictures of them together, to my sister in the middle of the damn night," Jaelynn answered for her.

He scrunched his face up. "What? Ky wouldn't do that."

"Ohhh, but he did. Jae, let's go. Tell your brother I'm done with his ass," Braelynn said with disgust.

"Hold up! I'm vouching for my brother. He wouldn't do that shit. You still got the text?" She nodded. "Let me see it."

She gave him her phone.

"Oh, hell naw. I'm telling you this can't be what it looks like. I know this looks..." He paused. "...compromising, but that nigga loves you."

He pressed something on her screen a few times, then gave the phone back to her.

"You should talk to him before jumping to conclusions," he pleaded on his brother's behalf.

"I'm good." she lied, knowing damn well her heart was breaking.

Braelynn and Jaelynn finally left and Kolby was still bothered by his brother's situation.

"Let me call this nigga and see what's up."

While he did that, I made a veggie burrito bowl for him and put it in the microwave, then put the leftovers in containers. I only heard bits and pieces of the conversation but it definitely sounded like Kyree was denying everything. Braelynn was completely in love with him, and it seemed like he was in love with her, too. All I could do was pray it worked out.

When Kolby got off the phone, he came into the kitchen. He approached me from behind, wrapping his arms around me and rubbing my stomach.

"Can I get a proper greeting, now that your company is gone?" he said as his lips grazed my neck.

I turned around and hugged him back. When he finished planting soft kisses along my neckline, he brought his lips to mine.

"I missed you," he said when our lips parted. "You're really starting to show." His hands caressed my stomach again.

"I missed you, too. And yeah, I'm gonna have to get more clothes soon."

"We can go shopping tomorrow."

"Okay. Are you hungry?"

"Starving. What'd you make?"

I went to the microwave and added a minute to the timer. The food was still warm so it didn't need much time.

"Veggie Burrito Bowls."

"Word? Sounds good. Did you eat?"

"Yes, I ate. I told you my appetite was better. Go sit down."

He went to the breakfast bar and sat while I waited for his food to finish in the microwave. When it was done, I took it out and sat it in front of him, with a fork. He didn't take his eyes off me the whole time.

"What do you want to drink, I have—"

"Water is good, baby."

I had to bend over to get the water out of the bottom of the fridge and when I stood, I felt a little pinch on my side.

"Ouch," I said, rubbing my side.

Kolby was off the stool and at my side so damn quick. With his hands holding my stomach he said, "What's wrong?"

"Calm down. Just growing pains." I laughed at his panicky ass, but he didn't find it funny.

"Come sit next to me. I should be the one serving you, anyway."

We went to the stools and I sat next to him while he ate. I couldn't help but wonder what it would be like if we were together every day.

"What's been up?" he said, breaking our silence.

I looked at him and laughed. "We talk and text every day all day. You know everything that's going on."

He chuckled. "I guess you're right." He ate a few more forkfuls before saying, "This is really good."

"Thank you. It's one of my favorite meals to make."

"Well, thank you for making it for me."

He finished his food and cleaned his dishes since I'd already done the rest. After making sure the door was locked and the alarm was set, he picked up his duffle bag and followed me to my room.

"What do you want to do tomorrow besides shopping? You taking me sightseeing?"

"I guess you haven't seen much of Seattle, huh? I'll look to see what's open on Sundays."

"Cool. C'mere and let me talk to my baby."

While he sat on the bench in front of my bed, I moved to stand between his legs. He lifted my shirt and planted kisses on my stomach.

"Hey, Baby Ross! We get to find out if you're a boy or a girl tomorrow. Mommy and Daddy don't care what you are. We just want you to be healthy. Have you been nice to Mommy while Daddy has been away? What's that? You have? Good job, baby. Daddy loves you."

I'd gotten used to him talking to my stomach, although this was the first time he did it in person. It still made me emotional but I managed to restrain my tears. He kissed my stomach a few more times and pulled my shirt back down. When he looked up at me, I saw something in his eyes. Something...different. I put both hands on his cheeks and leaned down to kiss him. His hands went to my ass and he moaned, causing me to pull away and look at him.

"That ass gettin' thick, My. Turn around and let me see if from the back."

He tapped my ass and tried to turn me around, but I pushed him and walk into my bathroom. I looked at my side view in the mirror, then turned with my ass and faced the mirror, then kissed my teeth.

"Shut up! My ass is not getting bigger."

I slammed the door on him and started the shower. I thought for sure he'd come and join me, but surprisingly, he didn't. When I went back to my bedroom, I saw why. His ass had fallen asleep.

"Kolby, wake up."

"Huh? What's up?"

"You fell asleep. Go shower so we can go to bed."

He sat up and stretched. "You know, I was doing some research about pregnancy and shit. I read that men can have pregnancy symptoms, too."

I laughed. "Which ones have you been having?"

"I've been exhausted. My ass be falling asleep at my desk at work. I've been going to bed earlier than usual. It's crazy."

"Welcome to my world. If I didn't work from home, I don't know how I would function."

He stood and kissed my forehead. "I'm about to shower. Don't fall asleep on me and don't bother putting no damn T-shirt on either."

If naked was how he wanted me, naked was how he was gon' get me. The number of times I'd used my vibrator in the past month was ridiculous. I'd never been this horny in my life. I had to change the batteries twice. He might not have been my man, but until I had this baby, his was mine.

KOLBY

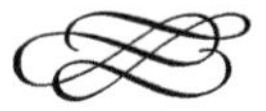

I figured Myla would be asleep when I was done showering, but she was wide awake, looking at her phone. I got in bed and slid next to her already-warm body.

"What are you looking at?"

"Some lingerie designs that Jaelynn sent me."

"When you gon' wear something for me."

"Eww! Me and my belly will pass on that."

She put her phone on the nightstand and turned to face me, putting her head on my chest. My fingers went to her head, and I gently massaged her scalp.

"I'm sure you would look beautiful, My. If not now, what about after you have the baby?"

I was trying to figure out a way to ask her if she wanted to make this shit official. This past month, I did a lot of thinking and came to a conclusion that, honestly, I already knew. Every time Myla and I talked, I tried to get a feel for where her head was, concerning us. We were having a baby, neither of us were seeing anyone else, and we were having sex. In many ways, it was like we were already a couple. I just needed to make sure we were on the same page.

"Umm, after I have the baby?"

"Yeah, when your six weeks is up."

She titled her head to look up at me. "I, uhh, I hadn't really thought that far. I wasn't sure if..."

"You weren't sure if what?"

"Kolby, what are we doing?"

"What do you want us to be doing?"

"That depends on what *you* want us to be doing?"

"I want you to be mine, as in my girlfriend, my woman, my lady, my significant other, my 'around the way girl', my main squeeze, all of it...along with the mother of my child."

"Soo...does that mean that you've changed your mind about being in a relationship...a long-distance relationship?"

"I changed my mind about being in a relationship with you while we were in Belize."

"What?"

"Yeah. Do you know how much I regret even saying that shit to you? By the end of that week, I was sprung."

"Good pussy will do that to you," she laughed, but that statement couldn't have been truer.

"I'm serious, My."

"Why didn't you say something?"

"Shit. You seemed cool with leaving everything in Belize and since I was the one that brought the shit up, a nigga didn't wanna get his feelings hurt."

She giggled a little, before straddling me. "Aww, the poor baby didn't wanna get his feelings hurt?"

She leaned down to place kisses all over my face. Her titties rubbed against my chest and her ass was tooted up in the air. This conversation was gon' have to be put on pause in a minute. My hands went to her ass and I gave it a gentle squeeze.

"Does this mean yes?" I asked, when I realized that she never answered my question.

"Kolby, I would love for us to try this out. I do care a lot about you, and I am having your baby. But we still live thousands of miles apart."

"Just tell me you'll be my woman and we will figure everything else out."

She looked to be seriously contemplating, and I was getting slightly annoyed.

"Are you *sure* you're not doing this just because of the baby?"

"Myla, I genuinely have feelings for you. I told you, my ass wanted to claim you as mine before we left Belize. I just wasn't sure if you were interested. Then when we got back, you kept replying to me with those dry-ass texts. I didn't know if you felt the same."

"Let's make a deal."

"What kind of deal?"

She pecked my lips, then each cheek, and followed that up with sucking on my neck, before she answered me.

"Let me blindfold you and tie up your hands."

She said that shit so casually, that I almost agreed without thinking.

"You wanna do what?"

"I want complete control. Blindfold and rope. If you let me do that, we can make this shit official."

"Damn, My. I had no idea you were this freaky."

"It's your baby's fault. I've never been this horny or freaky in my life. I want to suck the skin off your dick, then ride it until I pass out. But I don't want you to see or touch me while I'm doing it. Do we have a deal?"

This would definitely be something new for me. I've never given a woman complete control during sex. I guess there's a first time for everything.

"It's your world, baby."

She hopped off the bed with more excitement than I've ever seen her have.

"Be careful, woman. Hopping around with my baby like that."

"Boy, hush. You ain't gon' be saying shit when your dick is all up in my chest."

I nodded. "Good point."

She grabbed a little cloth bag out of her top drawer and came back to bed. From the bag, she removed a small rope and a blindfold.

"Kinda shit you been doing, My. I hope you ain't used this on no other nigga."

"You're the only man I've been with in over three years. Besides, I ordered this a couple of weeks ago, just for us. Now, scoot down some, and put this on."

She handed me the blindfold, and I took it from her cautiously.

"Don't do no crazy shit, My," I warned.

"I'm not. Just put it on, and lay down."

I moved down some on the bed, put the blindfold over my head, then pulled it over my eyes, before lying down.

"Put your arms above your head and your hands together."

"When did you become so bossy?" I teased, following her commands.

She straddled my waist and I could feel the heat radiating from her pussy. When she leaned forward to tie my wrists, her chest was right at my mouth. I couldn't help but to maneuver one of her titties into my mouth and suck on it. When she finished tying my wrists, instead of moving, she pressed her chest deeper and I opened my mouth wider.

Myla didn't have huge breasts, although they had gotten fuller since she'd been pregnant. I was trying to fit a whole one in my mouth. It was difficult without using my hands. I twirled my tongue around her nipple and sucked, causing her to moan and pull away.

"My bad, baby. I forgot you were in control." For about twenty seconds, I felt nothing. She was still straddling me, but she wasn't moving or touching me anywhere, which was making me anxious. "Baby, what—"

"Shh."

Finally, I felt her tongue gliding across my chest. She stopped at my left nipple and took it between her teeth, then gave my right nipple the same attention.

"Ssss," I hissed.

I could now feel the heat from her pussy over my dick and a moan slipped from my lips. I knew she was getting worked-up, because her breathing picked up and our connection became slicker.

"Ahh, shit! I'm cummin'," she mumbled against my chest.

I wanted to touch her so badly, so I wiggled my wrists to see if I could loosen the rope. She had that shit tied up real good because that didn't work.

I felt her lips graze my chest and she left a trail of kisses leading to my dick. I squeezed my toes together in anticipation of her taking me in her mouth. With her hand gripping the base, her tongue went around the tip.

"Argh!" I groaned.

Around and around and around, the tip of her tongue continued, before she finally let it travel down the full length. Up and down, up and down, up and down, then back around the tip and then—

"Shit!" I almost sat up when her mouth engulfed the head and she had half of it in her mouth.

She released her hand from the base and I could feel her head bobbing. As spit gathered, her mouth slid smoothly over my dick. When she added the suctioning of her jaws and picked up the pace, I almost lost it.

"Ahh, fuck, baby! Slow the fuck down."

Then she had the audacity to hum on the bitch. *What the fuck!*

"Baby, shit! Slow down or I'm gon' bust down your fuckin' throat."

That warning did nothing but encourage her. She began to gag, making her spit extra slippery. But her ass refused to slow down and I had no more fight left in me. She was about to swallow our baby's siblings.

"It's cummin', My. I'm about to blow."

Not being able to control the speed of her movements sent me completely over the edge, as semen began to shoot down her throat.

"Ahhhh, My! Shit! Fuuuccckkk!"

If she wasn't carrying my baby, I would have used my body to somehow toss her ass across the room. The grip she had on my dick with her mouth was like nothing I'd ever experienced. This no touching shit was about to go right out the window. My hands were still tied together, but I brought my arms to the front of my body and was about to try to push her head and force her to release her grip. As soon as I did that, she set my dick free, adding the 'pop' sound as she did so.

I was breathing so hard, it felt like my heart was about to jump out of my chest. Myla needed to get fucked real good after this stunt, and I planned to do just that as soon as I could get out of this rope.

"Myla, take this shit off."

"Not yet. Put your hands back above your head."

Unwillingly, I did as she asked; before my hands hit the bed, she'd slid her juicy pussy down on my dick.

"Ahhh," she screamed.

"Fucckkkk!" I shouted.

Not being able to see or use my hands brought out another side of me. I surprised myself with how vocal I was. Myla's hands went to my chest as she began to bounce up and down, then moved her hips in a circular motion. The moans, the groans, the cries, the sighs, the grunts...every verbal expression of appreciation that was possible, was passed between the two of us.

When I felt the throbbing of her pussy, I couldn't stand being in that rope another minute. I don't know how the fuck I broke out the shit but I did, then did away with the blindfold. Myla was too busy chasing her climax to notice. Her eyes were closed, head back, mouth open as she screamed my name.

"Kolbyyyy!" she screamed out when she felt my hands grip her waist, her head pop up and our eyes connected. She didn't object though. She couldn't. I immediately began to fuck her from the bottom and any words that she wanted to say got caught in her throat. Our simultaneous release had a nigga trying to figure out how to propose. She collapsed on my chest and fell asleep with my dick still snug inside of her.

MYLA

The nurse that was assigned to me on the day of our appointment was about to have me step outside of myself. During my visit last month, she seemed nice and was very professional. However, today, this bitch wanted to get choked up. I knew she was with the shits when she called us to the back. As soon as her eyes landed on Kolby, her whole demeanor changed.

She held the door open for us to walked through. Kolby held my hand as we approached the door, then placed his hand on the small of my back to allow me to enter first. Doing this put him right next to Nurse Hoe, and she said, "You smell heavenly."

"Umm, thank you," Kolby replied, uncomfortably.

"You're welcome," she said, cheesing and shit.

Kolby looked at me and shrugged his shoulders. After she took my weight, she led us to the examination room. As she was preparing to take my blood pressure, she said, "So, you're dad, huh?"

I didn't even let Kolby answer. "Yes, the fuck he is and don't address him again."

"Baby, calm down. Your blood pressure gon' be high as hell."

He rubbed my leg, trying to get me to relax. When she finished, my blood pressure was higher than normal and Nurse Hoe said, "Dr. Mavers will probably want to take your blood pressure again. Try not to get so worked up."

"Bi—"

"Can you just send the doctor in?" Kolby interrupted me.

"First, I need a urine sample."

She handed me the cup and I stepped down from the examination table. I didn't want to leave Kolby alone with Nurse Hoe so I said, "Come with me, baby."

Without hesitating, he followed me right on out the door and waited for me outside the bathroom. I knew I was doing too much but I didn't want to give that hoe a chance to be more disrespectful than she already had been. Especially, since I couldn't beat her ass like I wanted to.

I saw the smirk on her face when she walked back into the examination room. As soon as I handed her the urine sample, she left. I wanted to snatch her back by her phony ponytail.

I would definitely be requesting another nurse for future visits.

"She wants me to beat her ass," I said, still annoyed.

"You ain't beating nobody's ass while carrying my child. I don't even know why you lettin' her get to you."

"Cause she's disrespectful, that's why."

Before he could respond, Dr. Mavers walked in. She was a gorgeous, fifty-something year old Black woman. She'd been my gynecologist for about five years.

"Hey, Myla! Oh my! Is this handsome guy, dad?"

"Hey, Dr. Mavers. Yes, this is my boyfriend Kolby."

Kolby stood to greet Dr. Mavers and shook her hand.

"Nice to meet you, Doctor."

"You too, Kolby. Well, let's get started. How have you been feeling since your last visit?"

"Better. The morning sickness is pretty much gone. My appetite is improving."

She looked through my chart before saying anything else.

"It doesn't look like you've gained any weight and your blood pressure seems a little high."

"My, you told me you were eating more," Kolby said.

"I *have* been eating more. I don't know how I haven't gained weight. I feel like a cow already."

"Baby..."

"Myla, I assure you, you are far from a cow. If you haven't gained any weight by your next visit, I'm going to have to intervene. This isn't completely abnormal the first few months with the vomiting and loss of appetite. Now, let me check your blood pressure again; because that, I don't like to see."

Thankfully, it was back to normal and there was no cause for concern.

"I was probably a little too excited about finding out the sex of the baby."

"Ohh, that's right. This is that visit. Everything looks good. I'm going to check your urine sample and send the ultrasound tech in to set everything up."

"Wait. Is it the same nurse that was just in here?"

"Tanika? No. Why? Was there a problem?"

"She was flirting with Kolby. Can you make sure I have another nurse for the rest of my visits?"

"That damn girl. Excuse my language. I must admit, you're very handsome, but she knows better than that. No worries, I'll take care of it."

When Dr. Mavers left the examination room, I looked at over at Kolby, and he had a goofy grin on his face.

"What are you smiling about?"

"Your jealous ass."

"Who me? I'm nowhere near jealous."

"Yeah, okay. Why didn't you get mad when Dr. Mavers flirted with me?"

"Boy, Dr. Mavers was not flirting with you. She was just being nice."

"Maybe Tanika was just being nice. All she did was compliment my cologne and confirm that I was dad."

"Nigga, I know you saw how—"

Just then, the door opened and the ultrasound tech wheeled in a machine. She greeted us and proceeded to get everything set up. Shortly after, Dr. Mavers came back.

"I checked your urine sample and everything is good. Let's get started. Lay back, lift up your shirt, and push the waist band of your pants down."

Once I had done what she asked, Kolby kissed my stomach and took my hand. I looked at him and smiled. Dr. Mavers squeezed the cold gel onto my stomach and pressed the wand against it. I was beyond nervous and my hands were sweating. Kolby kissed my hand, then gave it a squeeze.

"Okay, so there's baby's heartbeat...and there's baby."

"Damn," Kolby whispered. "That's our baby."

I had forgotten that he wasn't here for the first ultrasound. When I looked at him, there were tears in eyes, which caused me to get teary-eyed.

"Wow! Will you look at that!" Dr. Mavers said, almost to herself.

I looked back at the screen and I didn't know what the hell I was looking at. Her comment, however, made me nervous.

"Is everything okay?"

"Is something wrong?"

Kolby and I asked at the same time. When Dr. Mavers turned to face us, the smile on her face calmed my nerves.

"Everything is fine. It looks like you two are having a girl...*and* a boy!" she said with a whole lot of excitement.

"We what?" Kolby asked.

"You're having *twins*!" she declared.

I couldn't speak. I literally couldn't find the words. *Twins?*

"Baby, say something."

"*Twins?*"

"Yes, twins! It looks like baby two was hiding behind baby one and their heartbeats were in sync. Look here."

We looked at the screen while Dr. Mavers pointed out each baby and their body parts. I couldn't believe my eyes.

"Do you have twins in your family?" she asked me.

"Uhh, yeah. My maternal grandmother; but her twin didn't make it."

"Well, there you have it. Looks like it skipped your mom and landed right on you. Everything else looks great. Here are new pictures for each of you with both babies. Congratulations!"

Kolby took the pictures from her and she left us in the examination room. Kolby stared down at the ultrasound with a huge smile on his face. My thoughts were all over the place, and I still couldn't wrap my head around this news. I cleaned myself up with the paper sheet that was tucked into my pants and Kolby helped me sit up.

"What are you thinking?" he asked.

"Honestly? I'm trying not to panic."

"Yeah, it's a lot to process. Are you excited?"

"The only thing I feel now, is shock. I need a minute to wrap my head around this. Two babies. I'm having two babies at the same time, Kolby. How am I supposed to do this? We're just barely in a relationship. You live in Chicago, I live here. I've never been a mother. How am I supposed to do this? I don't—"

"Baby, breathe! Calm down and breathe!"

Tears ran down my face and my breathing became labored. I was on the verge of a panic attack. He stood next to the examination table and pulled me into his arms, rubbing my back soothingly.

"You know you're not alone, right? I'll be here as much as I can, until we figure everything out, okay. We'll figure it out together."

A nurse, that wasn't Nurse Hoe returned to the room. By that time, Kolby had calmed me down. We finished up the appointment and the nurse gave me a bunch of literature about carrying multiples. I scheduled my next appointment and we left.

Kolby drove us back to my place, using the GPS. Although it was a short ride, I still managed to fall asleep. Once we got inside, all I wanted to do was go back to sleep but Kolby wouldn't let me do that until I ate. He warmed up the leftover veggie burrito bowls from the day before. After we ate, we took a nap.

When I woke up, Kolby's head and hand, rested just above my baby bump. He was sleeping so soundly, that I hated to wake him up, but my bladder was screaming.

"Baby, I need to use the bathroom," I said, tapping him as I spoke.

He moved to the pillow and I went to relieve myself. When I finished, I was headed out of the bedroom when I heard Kolby's voice.

"You're not coming back to bed?"

"I'm not tired anymore. I was gonna watch TV. It's still early."

"Can we talk first?" he asked, almost cautiously.

He got up and sat on the bench in front of the bed, and I did the same. He kissed my temple before he spoke.

"How you feeling about the babies now that you've slept on it?"

"It's still a lot to process, but I'm good. We just have a lot to figure out in a short about of time. They'll be here before we know it."

"Just know that we're in this together, okay? Don't ever feel like you're doing this alone." He touched my stomach. "That's us in there. God saw fit to give us two blessings; and as overwhelming as it seems, I'm grateful. There's no other woman that I'd want to experience this with. We got this."

When our lips connected, all of my reservations went away. This isn't the most ideal situation, but I was glad that I had a man like Kolby by my side, to help me get through it.

KOLBY

Two weeks had passed since we found out that we were having twins. Although it took Myla a while to process, she was now showing a lot of excitement. I was a little concerned the first few days after we learned the news. I had to fly back home the following day. I almost changed my flight but she convinced me that she was fine so I left. I had a feeling that she wanted to be alone.

Before the week was out, she sounded a lot better. She'd even bought a few outfits and other necessities for the babies. Each time we talked, she told me about something she read regarding having twins. I had to thank God for her change in attitude.

We decided not to tell anyone that we were having twins—at least not yet. Instead, we told them that the baby's legs were crossed and the doctor couldn't determine the gender. Everyone was under the assumption that we'd find out during our next visit, which was in two weeks.

In the meantime, Stella Ross, all but demanded that she meet Myla, in person. She told me that she was tired of FaceTime. Since my mother found out that the child that Kyree's ex was carrying wasn't his—like he'd suspected all along—she'd been more anxious than ever to meet Myla. She was one-click away from booking a flight, until I told her that Myla was coming for a visit. She would be staying until we had to fly back for her prenatal appointment. Thankfully, that got Stella off my back.

I was extremely nervous about her flying, but I called Dr. Mavers, and she assured me that it was safe for Myla to travel up until she reached about thirty-two weeks.

"Have you and Myla talked about permanent living arrangements, you know, since y'all official now and got a whole baby on the way?" Kamden asked.

Make that two babies.

"Not yet. I plan to do that while she's here. We're gonna go look at houses before she leaves."

He looked confused. "How the hell you gon' look at houses and you haven't even talked to her yet about moving here? If she's anything like Braelynn, good luck."

Braelynn had given my brother a hard time about moving to Chicago but now that they were engaged, she'd made plans to move.

"Our situation is a little different and I'm gon' talk to her before we look at the houses. I know better than that."

"I knew your ass was really feeling her when we were in Belize. I was surprised when you said y'all weren't keeping in touch."

I was a little hesitant to go into detail about having sex with Myla. If she was just some random, it wouldn't matter. We talked about randoms all the time. However, I had to tell somebody and my brothers were my best friends.

"Bruh, that shit was my fault. She was talking all that hot shit and my ass wanted fuck. I made sure that I told her before anything went down that I wasn't trying to have a relationship, especially not long distance. She was cool with it. Shit! Before the end of the week, I was sprung."

"You must have been, if you didn't wrap it up."

"That wasn't until the last night... but we had *two* rubbers break before that."

"Damn, bruh! She was meant to get pregnant."

When I didn't respond, Kamden gave me a questioning look. "What aren't you saying?" he asked.

I exhaled, then said, "Subconsciously, I think I may have gotten her pregnant on purpose."

"Bruuuhhh!"

"The rubbers that broke were from that little store they had on the resort grounds. I got the biggest ones they had but the shit was too small. I used them anyway and wasn't shocked or bothered when they broke."

"I ain't never in my life met a nigga that trapped a woman. Here's one... live and in person."

I shrugged my shoulders.

"Did you think she was on the pill?" he asked.

"Naw. I mean, she didn't say she if she was or wasn't, but she hadn't had sex in three years so—"

Kamden hopped out of his seat and put his fist over his mouth, as he shouted, "Whooaaaa! Three years bruh? That's why your ass was sprung. Three fuckin' years?" He sat back down, shaking his head.

"Then, that last night, I walked in on her in the shower. Next thing I know, I was shooting up the club."

"So, what you're saying is, y'all trapped each other? I ain't never heard no shit like this, bruh. Wouldn't it have been easier to just talk about your feelings? I swear, you and Kyree may be older, but y'all don't know shit when it comes to relationships." Kamden got up, shaking his head in disbelief.

We gave each other dap and a shoulder hug and he left. Myla would be flying in tomorrow, so I had to make sure it didn't look like two niggas lived here. Generally, Kamden and I kept our place clean, but women are particular about shit. I also needed to go grocery shopping, because we didn't have shit, as far as food.

As I was on my way out the door, my phone rang and Corette's name flashed across the screen.

"Shit!"

I didn't want to, nor did I have time to talk to her. I decided to let her go to voicemail and call her back tonight to let her know that our little fling was over. Right now, I had to get ready for my baby's visit.

MYLA

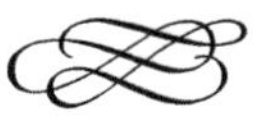

"Damn, I missed you," Kolby said, as he swooped me into a hug and kissed me.

When he put me back on my feet, his hands went to my stomach and he greeted his babies. He'd just picked me up from O'Hare Airport and we were headed to his parent's house.

"Daddy missed y'all, too. I heard y'all been in there fighting, giving Mommy a hard time."

I recently started to feel the babies move and sometimes if felt like they were having a wrestling match.

"You guys gotta keep it moving," the airport attendant yelled.

Kolby kissed my belly through the hoodie and tried to close my too-little jacket.

"Baby, I'm gon' get you a real coat that actually fits while you're here," he said with a laugh.

After putting my suitcase in the truck of his Ford Explorer, he helped me into the car.

"I had to talk my mother out of coming with me to the airport," Kolby said, once we were on our way.

"Oh, wow. She's so excited to meet me, I hope I don't disappoint."

"What? You could never be a disappointment. You're beautiful, intelligent, successful, friendly, and you're carrying her grandchildren. She probably already likes you more than she like her own children."

"I doubt it. I can tell when I talk to her on the phone that her boys are her heart."

"Do you how long she's been dropping hints about grandchildren? You're about to give her two... *and* one of them is a girl. Shit! We won't even exist when she finds that out."

I laughed. I knew that Kolby was just trying to calm my nerves. Even though I'd talked to Ms. Stella many times on the phone, meeting her in person was a whole different ball game.

As we drove to his parent's house, we talked about his job, my business, and the grand opening of Kyree's auto shop that was coming up soon. Because of Chicago traffic, the ride was long and at some point, I fell asleep. I woke up to an open passenger side door and Kolby kissing all over my face.

"Wake up, beautiful."

"I'm up."

He unlatched my seatbelt and waited for me to get my bearings, then helped me get out.

"I don't even remember falling asleep. This pregnancy got me feeling like a lazy bum."

"You're carrying two lives around inside of you. You have the right to be lazy, but you're not a bum, baby."

He let us inside his parent's home. There was a bunch of chatter in the family room, so we followed the noise. We found Kyree, Braelynn, Kamden, and who I assumed to be, Mr. and Mrs. Ross. Braelynn had been in town for a few days helping Kyree get ready for the grand opening. I was glad she was in town, and that I had someone to hang out with while I was here.

"Oh, my goodness, Myla is here."

Everyone looked in our direction as Ms. Stella rushed over to greet me, pushing Kolby out of the way. She gave me the warmest, most inviting hugs ever, making me feel right at home.

"Let me look at you. Take off your jacket, sweetheart. I wanna see you and my granddaughter."

"Hello to you too, Ma," Kolby said, as I took off my jacket. "And how do know it's a girl?"

"Because God wouldn't give me another one of you knucklehead boys. Awww, you are just gorgeous and I know you and my son made a beautiful baby. Come meet Kolby's father."

Mr. Isaac, who I only had the privilege of seeing on FaceTime a couple of times, stood from his recliner to give me a hug.

"It's nice to finally meet you. I was going to have to put my wife on a plane had this meeting taken any longer to happen. I tell you one thing. My boys sure do have good taste in women. I see I taught y'all well."

"Isaac, sit your behind down."

Mr. Isaac did as his wife told him, and I was finally able to greet my best friend, Kyree, and Kamden.

"Hey, sis. How was your flight?" Braelynn asked as we hugged.

"It was fine. I slept the whole flight, and half the ride here. What's up, Kyree? I had to fly all the way to Chicago to see my best friend. What kinda mess is that?"

I gave him a hug, as he replied, "Unless you moving here, too, you might as well get used to it."

"Yeah, whatever. Hey, Kam. I should have made Jae come with me," I teased as we hugged.

"Naw, you good. I keep trying to tell y'all, me and Jaelynn are just friends."

Everyone but his parents had something to say about that, all at the same time.

"Who is Jaelynn?" Ms. Stella asked.

"My younger sister. Her and your baby boy are in denial about their feelings for each other."

"I'm not in denial about shi—nothing. We're friends and y'all need to leave it alone."

He got up and left the family room. We all looked at each other with raised eyebrows, then Mr. Isaac said, "If they're just friends, it's not because that's all he wants to be. That's for sure."

We all agreed and moved on from the topic. Ms. Stella made lasagna, garlic bread, and salad for dinner. It was right on time because I was actually starving.

"Kolby, where's the bathroom?" I asked.

"I'll show you," he said, with a sneaky grin, as he led me down a short, dark hallway.

"Thank you. Can you make my plate? Your babies are hungry today."

"Of course," he replied, backing me against the wall. "You want everything?"

"Yeah, but don't put too much. I get full quick because I don't have a lot of room."

"Gimme a kiss."

I put my arm around his neck and we had a short make-out session. When he pulled away, he said, "I'm gon' fuck the shit outta you when we get to my place."

"I can't wait."

My hand moved to grip his dick, and he backed away.

"Are you trying to have me go back in that kitchen with a hard-on in front of my mama?"

"I just want to feel it right quick."

"Take your nasty, sexy, pregnant ass in the bathroom before I have you bent over the damn sink."

He roughly kissed my lips again, then left me there with moist panties.

When I went back to the dining room, everyone, including Kamden, was waiting for me so that Mr. Isaac could bless the food. After he said grace, we dug in.

"Girls, we need to have lunch and go shopping downtown while I have both of you here," Ms. Stella said.

"I'd love that," I said.

"Ms. Stella can shop, too, My," Braelynn said. "I hope you brought comfy shoes because we will be at the stores when the doors open and won't leave until the put us out."

"Braelynn, I thought we were better than that. I'm not that bad."

"Yes, you are, Dear. We know it and you know it," Mr. Isaac said.

I could do nothing but laugh. That's pretty much how the rest of the dinner went and I really enjoyed myself. When we finished, Braelynn and I offered to help clean up. Kolby tried to object on my behalf, but I told him I was fine. However, when we got to the kitchen, Ms. Stella and Braelynn insisted that I sit down. I knew there was no sense in arguing with them.

"So, Myla. Kolby didn't give me all the details of how you two came to be. He told me bits and pieces and I kind of filled in the blanks. Unlike Kyree and Braelynn, it wasn't love at first sight, was it?"

Oh shit. I should have listened to Kolby and took my ass in the family room.

When I didn't say anything, she said, "Sweetheart, we all grown up in here and I am not a judgmental person."

"She's really not, My. She knows I slept with Kyree after only knowing him for a few hours and I had a whole boyfriend at the time," Braelynn added, making me comfortable enough to share.

"It was more like lust at first sight. I had gotten to know him from afar while we were planning the trip. He seemed cool; I knew he was handsome because I'd seen pictures. But it wasn't until I saw him in person, that I kinda wanted to jump his bones."

Ms. Stella laughed.

"She hadn't had sex in three years, Ms. Stella," Braelynn volunteered my business.

"Whew, chile! I bet you did want to jump his bones."

"We kinda vibed with each other and by the end of the first night," I shrugged my shoulders. "We happened. But he made it clear before it happened, that he wasn't looking for a relationship. At that point, I was so horny, I would have agreed to anything."

"I know that's right!" Ms. Stella said, clapping her hands together. "After three years, I bet you were horny as hell."

"Then this happened," I pointed to my stomach. "I was afraid to tell him because I didn't want him to think I was trying to force a relationship. He reacted way better than I imagined."

"Which I told her would happen, because I knew he was raised right," Braelynn added her two cents.

"Well...tell me this," Ms. Stella began. "When did you fall in love with him?"

"Huh?"

Ms. Stella smiled and Braelynn's eyes got big.

"How long have you been in love with Kolby? Don't try to deny it because I can see it in your eyes when you look at him. I hear it in your voice when you talk to, or about him."

"Oh...I, umm...well–"

"He's in love with you, too," she said with confidence.

"Ms. Stella be knowing stuff, My. You can take her word," Braelynn assured me.

I didn't have anything to say because I was pondering her words. Ms. Stella let me be, as she and Braelynn, finished cleaning up. Kolby and Kyree came to see what was taking so long and Kamden called them whipped. Soon after, we were in the car and headed to Kolby's place.

"Did you enjoy your visit?" he asked.

"I did. Your parents are awesome. Must have been nice to grow up seeing that kind of love between the two people that created you."

"They're definitely goals."

He took his eyes off the road briefly and caught me staring at him. Taking my hand in his, he brought it to his lips as he focused on the road. I was still stuck on the end of my conversation with Ms. Stella. I'd been trying to avoid my real feelings for Kolby, telling myself that we were the way we were, because of the babies. She brought those bitches right to the forefront of my mind.

Once inside of him and Kamden's three-bedroom apartment, he gave me a quick tour. They used the third bedroom as an office and workout room. The décor was typical for a male bachelor pad. I couldn't help but wonder how Kolby was going to adapt to be a father of two, in a matter of months. When we got to his bedroom, I looked around and couldn't help but wonder if he was the type of nigga that brought his random fucks back to his house.

"Is this where you bring all of your women to snatch their souls?" I asked casually.

"Is that your way of trying to find out if I've fucked anyone else in this bed?"

He had gone into his walk-in closet and walked out shirtless, with a smirk on his face.

"You think you know me?" I paused, trying not to crack a smile. "But yeah...do I need to sleep on the couch?"

We both laughed as he put his hands on my stomach and kissed my forehead.

"First of all, I would never disrespect you and my seeds like that. Secondly, don't take this the wrong way, but women are crazy. The first thing my dad told us when we moved out, was to never let a woman know where you lay your head, unless you're in a serious relationship; and I've never had one of those."

"Smart man."

"That means, your soul will be the first, last, and only one being snatched while in this bed."

Hearing him say that made my heart smile. If I was light-skinned, he would have seen me blushing.

A little while later, I had showered and was in a pair of leggings and a t-shirt, sitting on Kolby's bed while he showered. His phone was on the dresser and it began to vibrate. I ignored the buzzing initially, but it continued for a good two minutes. I got up to silence it and saw the name Corette on the screen. When the call went to voicemail, I saw that she had called and texted several times.

Who the fuck is Corette?

By the time Kolby got out of the shower, I was pretending to be asleep. He got in bed and pulled me into his chest.

"Why are you wearing this T-shirt?" he asked, before nuzzling his nose into my neck.

"I'm tired."

"Too tired for some of this?" He rubbed his hard dick against my bare ass.

"It's been a long day."

If his phone hadn't vibrated again, he would have persisted. Instead, he got out of bed and retrieved his phone. I heard his dresser drawer open and close, then seconds later, he left the room. When I heard the door close, I looked on the dresser to see that he'd taken his phone with him.

It was ten o'clock here but in Seattle, it was only eight. Since I'd taken two naps today, I actually wasn't tired at all. Not even an hour ago, my mind was consumed with facing my true feelings for Kolby. Now, I'm trying to figure out if the nigga was playing me.

KOLBY

Last night, when I got out of the shower, my dick was already hard. *We...* as in me and my dick... had been looking forward to sliding inside Myla's walls since the last time we were there. Everything was cool before my shower, but when I got out, shit was downright cold. However, when my phone vibrated and I saw Corette's name, then peeped how many times she'd called and texted, I wondered if Myla's change in attitude was because she'd peeped the same thing.

I left the room and called Corette back. She had been blowing me up for the past couple of days and I intended to call and let her know what we had going on, was over. With all the prepping I did for Myla's arrival, I forgot to call. Now, here I am, with my pissed-off pregnant girl in my bed, sneaking to call her back. Corette was cool and I respected her, so I wanted to end things amicably. I thought it would be a quick and easy conversation.

"Finally!" she answered.

"Yeah, my bad. I've been kinda busy. Wassup?"

"I told you I'd be in Chicago. I'm flying back out in a couple of days and I wanted to see if you wanted to hook up before I leave."

"Corette, a lot has changed in the past few months. I'm in a relationship now and—"

"A relationship? The man who is opposed to relationships, is in a relationship? Wow!"

"Yeah. So, that being said. We can't hook up."

"So, you're serious, serious. You know I don't care if you fuck other people. We ain't never been on that. I just thought—"

"I'm serious, and things with my girl are serious."

"Were y'all serious when I told you I'd be in town?"

"Not officially, but we were moving in that direction."

"Kolby, I—"

"Look, Corette, I wasn't trying to have a long, drawn out conversation about this. I gotta go. You take care."

I ended the call and blocked her number. When I went back to my room, Myla was snoring softly. I crawled in bed behind her and pulled her to my chest. She snuggled against me, which meant her ass was sleep for real, since she'd given me her ass to kiss ten minutes ago. I fell asleep with her in my arms, knowing that damage control would be necessary.

This morning, I woke up in bed alone. After taking care of my morning hygiene, I found her sitting on the couch talking to Kamden. When she saw me, her whole demeanor changed and she got quiet. She literally stopped talking mid-sentence.

Kamden looked back and forth between us and said, "Aww, shit. I'm out. Myla, take care of my niece or nephew while I'm gone."

"Bye, Kam," she said.

I took Kamden's place on the couch and Myla kept her face buried in her phone.

"Did you eat?" I asked her.

"Yeah."

"What'd you eat?"

"Food."

"Baby—"

Her head shot up from her phone and she gave me an evil glare.

"Don't 'baby' me! Who the fuck is Corette, and why the fuck was she blowing up your phone?"

That didn't take long.

"If you wanted to know who she was, all you had to do was ask. All this attitude ain't necessary."

"Answer my damn questions."

"She's somebody I used to fuck around with."

"Are you still fucking her?"

"I said *used to*. Why would you ask me some shit like that?"

"Because I wanna know. Are you?"

"No, baby, I'm not. She's a flight attendant and she doesn't even live in Chicago."

"Oh, so if she lived in Chicago, y'all would still be fucking?"

"What? No! That's not what I meant."

"Sounded that way to me. Why would she feel it was necessary to call and text you back-to-back like that?"

"I don't know. You would have to ask her."

"I don't want to ask her. I'm asking my man, and the father of my children. If we still talking to exes and people we used to fuck, let me know so I can act accordingly."

"Myla, don't get some nigga fucked up while you playing."

"Ain't nobody playing. I know you called her back. What did she want?"

"Why does that even matter, baby? I told her that I was in a relationship and I already blocked her number, so she won't be calling again."

"What—did—she—want?" she asked between clenched teeth.

I had never seen Myla this pissed, and if I answer that question, it wasn't gonna help this situation much. Thankfully, there was a knock on the door that halted our conversation. While I went to answer the door, she stomped back to my bedroom, slamming the door behind her.

"Who is it?" I asked before I reach the peephole.

Nobody said anything and when I looked out the peephole, no one was there. I opened the door to see if someone had left a package. As soon as I pulled it open, I regretted it. Before I realized what the fuck was happening, Corette pushed the door open and forced her way inside.

"Corette, what the hell are you doing here?" I whispered through my teeth. I stood in front of the door to keep it open.

"I came to see you."

"Why? I told you last night that I'm in a relationship. You gotta go!"

"I told you last night that I don't care. Are you really about to pass up on all this?"

She opened the black trench coat that she had on and underneath...*got damn!* She had on the sexiest red, lace panty and bra set. *Shit!*

Corette was a tall, lean, chocolate woman with short, naturally curly hair. At some point, she wanted to be a model; I had no doubt that had she seriously pursued it, she would have been successful. I'm sure she told me at some point, but I can't remember, how she became a flight attendant. We met on a flight and she was spending the night in Chicago. From that point on, whenever she was in town, she'd hit me up.

"Corette, close your damn coat and take your ass on."

"You're a persistent ass hoe," Myla shouted from the hallway.

She walked toward us, with one hand on her stomach. I rushed to her side, taking her other hand.

"Baby, I swear to God—"

"Is she the reason you cut me off?" Corette interrupted.

"I told you—"

"Yes, bitch! Me and the twins we're having. Now take your desperate ass on somewhere."

"For real, C. You need to go. I told you what was up last night."

Corette's eyes focused in on Myla's stomach, then she looked at me, before her eyes connected with Myla's angry ones.

"Clearly, you didn't mind sharing him back in July. Why you being stingy now?"

"If I wasn't pregnant, I'd beat the bricks off your ass," Myla snapped.

"If you weren't pregnant, you wouldn't even be here. He's just trying to do the right thing. Relationships ain't for him," Corette spat back, before yanking the door open and walking out.

As soon as the door slammed closed, Myla yanked her hand away from me and marched to my bedroom, slamming the door behind her again. I hesitantly followed, and when I twisted the knob to enter the room, the door was locked.

"Myla, baby, open the door, please."

"You lied to me, Kolby. Twice! You lied to me when you really didn't have to!"

Lied to her. I didn't lie about anything.

"What are you talking about? I told you who she was."

I heard her fumbling with the knob and the door opened. I was prepared to walk in but she came out, dragging her suitcase on wheels behind her. She had on one of my hoodies with the hood over her head and her too-little jacket on.

"Where you going?"

"Away from your lying ass."

"Myla, stop fuckin' playin' with me."

I pulled her suitcase from her hand and she stopped walking to turn around and face me.

"Kolby, I really can't be around you right now. It's not good for me and it's not good for the babies. Give me my suitcase and let me leave."

"Baby, tell me what I lied about." I took a step toward her and she put her hand up.

"You probably don't even remember because the lie slipped off your tongue so easily."

"You asked who she was and I told you. I didn't have a chance to tell you what she wanted because she knocked on the door. When did I lie?"

"Were y'all in a relationship?"

"Hell, naw!"

"Then how does she know where you live?"

Shit! I forgot that I brought Corette back here once. I'd picked her up from the airport and Kamden had left something in my car that I had to bring to him. She begged to come inside and I ended up showing her the place.

When I didn't say anything, she kept on. "Annddd, I asked you, straight up, if you fucked anybody else after Belize and you said no. That bitch just said y'all fucked in July."

Shit! I didn't catch that.

"Baby, I forgot—"

"Really, Kolby. You're about to stand there and tell me you forgot you brought a woman to your apartment, and that you forgot that you fucked the same woman a few months ago."

Umm...

"Give me my suitcase."

"No! You're not leaving. You don't know shit about this city."

"Fine!"

I watched her walk out the door, thinking that she was just calling my bluff. Myla couldn't go anywhere but the hallway. She didn't have a car and only knew my family. Once she realized that, she'd have her ass right back in this apartment. I'd give her a minute to cool off but after that, I'd carry her back inside if I had to.

Who am I fooling?

Thirty seconds hadn't passed and my ass was out the door. Myla wasn't in the hallway, so I went to the main entrance of the building. As I stepped onto the sidewalk, I caught a glimpse of Myla getting into a car.

"Myla? What the fuck, baby?" I shouted.

She probably didn't hear me because the door closed and the car drove off. *I done fucked up!*

MYLA

There wasn't a word in the dictionary to describe how angry I was with Kolby. I kept replaying everything that had just happened, wishing that I could just wipe it out of my mind. Kolby and I weren't together in July, so I wasn't upset that he slept with ole girl, or anyone else, for that matter. He was free to sleep with whoever he wanted. I was upset because I asked him about it and he lied. Lying about it was so unnecessary.

That was minor, though, compared to the real nerve that Corette struck. I'd battled with the question for several days after we became official. I thought I'd buried the insecurities surrounding it. Looks like they are very much still present. Maybe I needed to face the reality that if I wasn't pregnant, there would be no Kolby and Myla. *Was he lying when he said he had genuine feelings for me?*

My phone vibrated in my hand and I answered Braelynn's call.

"Hey."

"My, don't 'hey' me. Why the hell is Kolby about to put an APB out on your ass? Where are you going?"

"His mom is meeting me at their house. Don't tell Kolby,

though. Let his ass worry. And don't tell Kyree because you know he'll snitch."

"Well, you're lucky he's not here. Seriously, though, what happened?"

"Honestly, Brae, I don't feel like talking about it right now. And promise me you won't tell anyone where I am?"

"I promise. As long as I know you're safe. Love you!"

"Love you, too."

"Ma'am, we're here," the Uber driver said.

"Okay. Thank you."

I got out and made my way to the front door of Mr. and Mrs. Ross' house. Thankfully, when I sent her the text, I'd caught her home for an early lunch, and she agreed to wait for me to get there. She opened the door for me, and could immediately tell that all was not well.

"What the hell did my son do?" she asked as she closed the door.

I waited to see what room she would go to, then followed her into the kitchen. She sat at the table and I sat across from her.

"Talk to me, sweetheart."

"I'm sorry for interrupting your day."

"Don't worry about it. Now, what's wrong?"

I exhaled deeply before I began. "Last night, Kolby was in the shower. His phone was on the dresser vibrating, like someone was calling and texting him repeatedly, back to back. I ignored it for a while but when it continued, I got up to see who was calling. Honestly, I thought it may have been an emergency. I didn't touch his phone or go through it, because I'm not that kind of girl. I saw the name Corette scrolling across the screen and she'd called and texted multiple times.

Ms. Stella gave me all of her attention as I told her everything that happened. By the time I was done, my face was wet with tears. She reached across the table for my hands before speaking.

"Myla, didn't I tell you yesterday that my son was in love with you?"

"Yes, ma'am."

"Do you think I said that just to hear myself talk?"

"Well, no, but—"

"There is no but. I only speak things that I know to be true. Things that I'm told by the good Lord, Himself. If Kolby's heart would have been open to love when y'all got together in Belize, he would have fallen head over heels for you right then and there. But he and Kyree are so different, in that way. Once Kyree was reunited with Braelynn, he was ready to embrace the love he felt for her. Kolby, he's more cautious with his feelings. Things have to make sense for him."

"Before Corette left, she said something that hit me deep."

"What was that, sweetheart?'

"She said...if I wasn't pregnant, I wouldn't be here, and that Kolby is just trying to do the right thing."

"Oh, baby girl, is that what you think?"

"Sometimes."

"Does Kolby's actions make you feel like the sole reason he's with you is because of the baby?"

"Well, no, but—"

"I done already told you there are no buts. What does his actions say?"

"Kolby is the most loving and caring man I've ever been with. From the moment he found out that I was pregnant, he's been the so...perfect. His actions made it so easy to fall in love with him."

"Then don't let some lil' skank come in and plant seeds of doubt. Listen, it may seem like he's only here for the baby, but you getting pregnant was the extra push he needed to follow his heart. Believe me, baby girl, he would have eventually made his way to you."

Talking to Ms. Stella made me feel a lot better. Before she went back to work, she insisted on heating me up a plate of leftovers.

"Let me go get my phone out of my purse. I'm willing to bet your man has been calling," Ms. Stella said.

When she came back to the kitchen, she was holding her phone as she waited for the person she called to pick. It was on speaker because I could hear it ringing.

"Ma, Myla left and she's not answering her phone!" Kolby sounded panicked on the other end of the line.

"What do you mean she left? What happened?"

"This girl I used to mess around with was blowing up my phone last night, and popped up over here this morning. Her and Myla exchanged some words and after Corette left, Myla did, too. Ma, she don't know nobody out here. I called Kyree and Braelynn hasn't heard from her. Kam is at work. I need to find her and make sure her and the babies are okay."

Oh shit!

"Calm down, Kolby. Wait, did you say babies? She's having twins?"

"Oh, damn! We were keeping that a secret," Kolby said.

"I can't believe y'all kept a secret like this from me. I'm so hurt. I'm at work, son. I gotta go."

"Ma—"

The call ended and I could feel Ms. Stella's eyes on me. I kept my face in my plate and I felt her approaching me.

"Boy, this lasagna is even better the next day. You really put your foot in—"

"Myla Abbott, you just sat here and cried in my arms and you've been keeping this big secret from me."

I slowly lifted my head until my eyes met hers.

"Sorry," was all I could think to say.

"Get your butt up outta that chair and give me a hug. You're giving me two grandbabies?"

When I stood, she wrapped her arms around me in the best hug ever. A hug that I really needed. She released me, looked at me with pleading eyes and said, "Please, tell me at least *one* of them is a girl."

"One of each."

Her arms went back around me as she shouted like she'd just hit the jackpot at the casino. When she finally let me go, she danced around the kitchen as she continued shouting, "God is good, all the time. All the time, God is good."

"Myla, you just made my day, girl. You made my year. I can't wait to tell all my friends. Oh, I gotta get back to work. I ain't doing nothing else today, though. Gonna look online and get my grandbabies some matching outfits."

"Ms. Stella, can you keep it under wraps for a little while? We haven't told anybody."

She looked at me like I had shit on my face.

"Are you crazy? I can't hold on to information like this."

"Please, Ms. Stella. I know you're excited but we wanted it to be a surprise."

"Whew, chile! You asking a lot right now."

She took a deep breath and she shook her head in disbelief.

"Fine!" she conceded. "They are *your* babies and you should be able to decide how and when you want to tell everyone."

"Thank you!" I hugged her and kissed her cheek.

"Yeah. Let me get back to work. You okay now?"

"I'm fine. Thank you for listening."

"I'm always here for you, Myla. You and my grandbabies." Her smile was huge when she mentioned the babies. "Call my son, please. At least let him know you're okay before he has a heart attack. You can stay as long as you want. Kyree's old room is the second door on the left, if you want to take a nap. Oh, and if you leave before me or my husband gets home, just lock the bottom lock."

"Okay. Thank you!"

Ms. Stella left and I finished eating my food. After cleaning my dishes, I looked at my phone to see that Kolby had called fifty-three times and sent almost as many text messages. I wasn't ready to engage with him, but I sent him a text to let him know I was fine and I'd be there later. I knew he'd start calling and texting again, but my phone was on silent, so it didn't bother me as I went to his old room to take a nap.

KOLBY

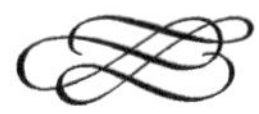

For a minute, Myla had me about to lose it. Eventually, I calmed down. She's a smart and resourceful woman and I knew she wouldn't do anything to put herself or our babies at risk. Braelynn said that she had spoken with her, but Myla didn't let on where she was headed; my mother was of no help either. When I slipped up and told her we were having twins, she hung up in my face.

A text came through from Myla telling me that she was okay, and when I replied back to her, she left me on read. Suddenly, I remembered something that I should have thought of hours ago. The last time I was in Seattle, she shared her location with me before she left to run an errand. I went to her text and when I saw where she was, I felt dumb as hell. Throwing on a hoodie and grabbing my car keys, I left my apartment. Once my car connected to the Bluetooth, I called my mom for the second time.

"You're lucky I'm even answering your call! How could you keep such a big secret from me?"

"How could you not tell me that Myla was at your house when you heard how worried I was?"

"Don't change the subject!"

"My bad, Ma. We were trying to surprise everybody."

"Yeah, yeah, yeah. She already told me and I agreed not to say anything, but y'all owe me big time for keeping this secret."

"Thanks, Ma. Now, back to my question."

"You know what? My boss is calling me. I gotta go. Love you, son." She hung up on me again.

Ten minutes later, I walked into my parent's house. It was quiet but I could smell lasagna. Checking the kitchen, I saw that no one was there. The family room was empty as well. Just as I was thinking she may have left, I peeked inside my old room and there she was.

For about five minutes, I leaned on the doorframe and watched her sleep. She looked so peaceful and unbothered. Instead of waking her, I kicked off my shoes and got in bed with her. I positioned myself behind her on the full-sized bed and pulled her close, resting my hand on her stomach. I sighed with relief when she snuggled up next to me.

I heard Myla's voice and my eyes popped open. It felt like only five minutes had passed, but it had to be more. Only a bit of light peeked through the curtains.

"Why are you here?" she repeated.

We were lying face-to-face, with our noses almost touching.

"When I figured out where you were, I came to get you."

"What if I don't want to leave with you?"

"You can stay but my babies are coming with me."

She laughed and pushed my shoulder.

"They can't go without me."

"I guess you gotta bring your ass, too. Baby, I don't want to fight anymore."

"Why'd you lie?"

"Baby, I really had forgotten that Corette had ever been there."

I went on to explain to her why Corette had ever been in our apartment and assured her that we did not have sex there.

"Why'd you lie about not sleeping with anyone after Belize?"

"I wouldn't say that I lied."

"But what you said made it sound like you hadn't been with anyone else. You could have been up front with me. I wasn't expecting you to sit around saving yourself for me."

"What I said was true. After being with you in Belize, I couldn't think about anybody else. Corette hit me up and asked me to meet her for drinks at her hotel. I agreed and we ended up fucking. I regretted that shit immediately, because she wasn't you. I'm sorry for not being completely honest with you."

"We weren't a couple at the time, so it was pointless for you to lie, Kolby."

"It was, and I can't tell you why I did. I just know that I'm sorry."

She let me kiss her lips and I felt like I was making progress.

"Can I ask you something else?"

"Anything."

"If I wasn't pregnant, do you think we'd be together?"

I knew the shit Corette said got to her.

"Didn't we already discuss this? Don't ever let a woman that would do anything to be in your position, make you feel insecure about your place in my life. And just so we're clear, my sole purpose for coming to Seattle with my brother that day, was to get to you. I had no idea that you were carrying my seeds."

She didn't say anything but I wanted to clear her mind of any doubts she had about me and my feelings for her.

"I love you, Myla. And not because you're having my children. The fact that you're carrying not one, but two of my seeds, makes me love you even more. But falling in love with you...baby, you made it easy."

She smiled and connected her lips with mine for a quick kiss.

"You want to hear something funny?"

"What I want is to bury my face between your thighs. Can I do that?"

"Kolby?"

"Okay, fine. Tell me something funny."

"I told your mom earlier today that you were easy to fall in love with."

"You're in love with me, Myla."

"Head over heels."

"That makes me want to bury my face between your thighs, drain you of all your womanly fluids, then plunge my dick so deep inside of you that the twins think they have another sibling in there."

"Shit!"

"Can I do that?"

"Please."

I didn't hear any movement on the other side of the door but I got up and locked it anyway. The last thing I needed was for one of my parents to see me blowing Myla's back out. She had already taken off her leggings and was in the process of taking off my hoodie. I took all my shit off in a hurry and rejoined her in the bed.

"Why didn't you take this off?" I said as I unhooked her bra. She must have slid her underwear off with her leggings.

"Because my boobs are so sensitive and heavy."

"I'm sorry, baby. Let me kiss them for you."

My body was positioned on the side of her because her stomach wouldn't allow it me to be on top. Taking one of her breasts in my hand, I could feel the heaviness. I leaned in and twirled my tongue around her nipple, before covering her whole areola with my mouth.

"Ssss!" she hissed.

While my mouth gave each of her breasts its full attention, my hand went between her legs. Her slick fluid was already seeping out and I was anxious to get a taste. I moved to hover over her body as my mouth made its way down to her stomach.

"Daddy need y'all to behave while he makes mommy feel good," I said before showering her belly with kisses.

When I was face-to-face with what I call my slice of heaven, my mouth watered. I put her legs on my shoulders and latched on to her clit. Her sticky juices coated my tongue as I lapped it up.

"Shit, baby," she tried to whisper but it came out much louder.

I flicked my tongue up, down, and around her pussy, sucking up her juices as she got wetter. Upon her explosion, my entire mouth smothered her hot box and I damn near choked on her sweet nectar. She used one of the pillows to muffle her screams.

Hovering above her again, with all of my weight on my arms, I allowed her to taste herself on my lips and tongue in a sloppy, wet kiss.

"Turn around and get on your knees," I said when I pulled my mouth away from hers.

I moved back and watched her do as I asked. With the little bit of light that came through the window, I could see Myla's beautiful ass tooted up in the air. I got on my knees behind her and put my hands on her sides. I couldn't get a grip on her waist like I wanted, but I was gon' make this shit work.

Gliding inside of her, we both released a sigh. Whoever said pregnant pussy was the best ain't never told a muthafuckin' lie. I had to get my head right before I gave her the first stroke.

"Hurry up, baby."

"Girl, this pussy too good to rush. If I hurry up, my nut gon' hurry out."

I gripped her shoulder and finally slid my dick out, before ramming it back inside.

"Uhn," she moaned.

I did that a few times, nice and slow, before keeping a nice even pace. Her pussy felt so good, I no longer cared if Stella and Isaac were home.

"Fuuucckk, My!" I groaned between clenched teeth.

I reached around and underneath her belly and placed two fingers on her clit. The more I massaged, the wetter her pussy felt around my dick.

"Kol—by, I'm 'bout—to—cum!"

Right away, her walls clenched around my shit and siphoned out every ounce of nut in my dick. If my parents were home, they would surely be scarred for life after hearing all the sounds that came when we released, simultaneously.

MYLA

A week had passed since Kolby and I had our first argument. Things had been great but I'd been avoiding his parents. They heard us having sex in Kolby's childhood room and I was still embarrassed. Braelynn and I were going shopping with Ms. Stella, so I had to get over my embarrassment.

Kolby and Kamden were both at work and I was in their apartment alone. It had been that way for the past few weekdays. After I finished getting dressed for our shopping outing, I FaceTimed my mom. We'd been texting every day that I'd been there but I hadn't talked to her. I'd been debating on telling her about the twins since Ms. Stella found out.

"Hey, daughter!"

"Hey, Mommy!"

"How are you and my grandbaby feeling? Let me see your stomach."

I was sitting on the couch and I lifted the sweater to show her my belly.

"Aww, look at youuu," she sang. "Boy, you're really poking out there."

"I know. I'm gonna be a cow soon."

"Girl, cut it out. You're beautiful. So, how is everything else?"

"Everything is good."

"You sure? You sound kinda down."

"Well, last week, the day I got here, Kolby and I kinda got into it before we went to bed. The next morning, I ended up taking an Uber to his mom's house."

"Myla, Chicago is a dangerous city, and you don't know your way around. What is wrong with you?"

"Chicago is no worse than any other city. Anyway, he and his parents live in good neighborhoods."

"Well, what was it about that made you leave?" she asked. I could hear the concern in her voice.

I explained it all to her and she understood why I was upset, but didn't agree with me leaving.

"You two share a child and you can't leave every time something happens, Myla."

"I know, Mommy. I shouldn't have let that hoe bother me."

"Well, hoes will always be hoes, sweetheart. But I trust that Kolby is a good man, and he wouldn't do anything to jeopardize your relationship."

"He told me he loved me."

"Oh, did he? How do you feel about him?"

"I love him, too. Mommy, he is the sweetest, kindest, sexiest, finest, man I've ever met. I don't know how I got so lucky."

"Aww, I'm happy for you sweetheart. Maybe you two will get married soon. Have you talked about that?"

"We live two thousand miles away from each other. We need to figure that out before we talk about marriage."

"Honey, I already know you'll be living in Chicago. I'm trying to mentally prepare myself to be a long-distance grandmother."

I could hear the sadness in her voice, which made me feel bad because she was probably right. Although Kolby and I hadn't talked about me moving here, I had a feeling he'd bring it up soon.

"Aww, Mommy. Don't make me feel bad. If that happens, I'll make sure we FaceTime every day and visit often."

"Don't worry about me. You live your life sweetie. What are your plans for today?"

"Brae and I are going shopping with Ms. Stella, Kolby's mom. I was actually calling you to tell you something. You have to promise me you won't get too upset."

"I can't make any promises. You're scaring me now."

"It's nothing like that. I just...I'm having twins, Mommy. A boy and a girl."

Her hand flew over her mother and she hopped around her kitchen. I let her have a few minutes to process, because I knew it was a lot. When she focused back on the screen, she had tears in her eyes.

"Myla, why would I be upset? This is wonderful news. Twins. I can't believe it. I always forget that my mother had a twin... and that it's even a possibility."

"We wanted to keep it a secret and surprise everyone, you know, like Sondra and Elvin did on *The Cosby Show*. But Kolby accidently told his mom, so I had to tell you."

"I don't give two shits about who found out first, I'm too excited to care. Can I tell your brother?"

"No, Mommy, please. We're gonna figure out a way to tell everyone else. I know he's gonna be mad that I didn't tell him right away, but he'll get over it. Kolby and I will make the official announcement soon. As of now, only you and Ms. Stella know."

"Okay, sweetheart. I'll text you later. Have fun shopping. Love you."

"Love you, too, Mommy."

After ending the call, I rubbed my stomach and said to the babies, "I guess it's time we tell the world that there's two of you."

I got up to use the bathroom because Braelynn had sent a text saying they were six minutes away. By the time I walked out of the building, she was pulling up with Ms. Stella in the passenger seat.

As I approached the truck, Ms. Stella got out. She gave me a hug then helped me into the back seat.

"Hey, sis! If you weren't pregos and it wasn't so cold, we'd use public transportation, so you could get the real Chi-town experience," Braelynn said.

"Listen to you. Trying to sound like this your city. You ain't officially moved yet," I teased.

"I know, but I've been here so much that it already feels like home. How is the baby?"

Before I could answer, Ms. Stella cleared her throat.

"The baby is fine. We have our six-month appointment when I go back."

"Maybe the baby will cooperate this time, so I'll know if I'm having a niece or nephew."

Ms. Stella cleared her throat again.

There is no way she's gonna be able to keep this a secret for much longer.

"Yeah, hopefully."

We talked about a little of everything on the way to downtown Chicago. When we got there, we parked in one of the parking garages and I couldn't believe how expensive it was. I was almost mad that we didn't take public transportation.

It was cold outside and I was glad that Kolby bought me a heavier and bigger coat. We were in and out of stores all day and Ms. Stella had to have some packages mailed to her house. Braelynn was not lying when she said that this woman could shop.

By the time we left, Kolby had called all three of us multiple times and threatened to come pick me up, if they didn't hurry up and bring me home. I was so tired that I fell asleep before we left the parking garage. When I opened my eyes again, Kolby was planting kisses on my stomach.

"Daddy's babies good in there? Mommy, grandma, and Titi Braelynn have all lost their minds. Y'all are probably exhausted with all the moving around Mommy did today," he said to the twins.

"What are you doing?" I asked.

"I'm trying to make sure my babies are good. My mom and Braelynn had you out entirely too long. I had to carry you from the car to the bed, took off all your clothes, and tucked you in. You didn't bat an eye until I started talking to my kids."

I yawned. "It was a long day. Your mom sure can shop."

He shook his head. "They should be ashamed of themselves. You've been on your feet for like ten hours. I'm about to call my mom and—"

"Baby, I'm fine. Don't risk your life talking to your mom crazy. I felt good while we were out and we rested whenever I needed to. Chill out."

"What are you doing?" he asked when I got out of bed.

"I have to pee and then I'm gonna wash my face and brush my teeth. Is that okay, Daddy?"

He mumbled something under his breath as I walked away. *Big ole baby.* He was already in bed when I returned. I turned the lamp off and snuggled up against him.

"I missed you," he said.

"Aww, baby. I missed you, too."

"I took tomorrow off. I made plans for us, if you're not too tired."

I couldn't see his face but he sounded like he was pouting. *Big ole spoiled baby.*

"I won't be tired. So...I told my mom about the babies today."

"That's cool. What'd she say?"

"She was excited and shed a few tears. I was thinking maybe we should make the announcement."

"Whatever you wanna do, baby."

"Can we have everyone over tomorrow? I can have my mom, brother, and Jaelynn on FaceTime. Maybe I can cook—"

"Oh, hell naw. After you were on your feet all day today. You ain't cooking shit. I'll order their asses some pizza."

"But—"

"I said what I said, My. They like pizza. If they don't want that, they can eat elsewhere. I'll send a group text to everyone in the morning."

"Okay, baby. Goodnight."

"Goodnight. I love you."

"I love you."

We pecked each other's lips and within minutes, I was in dreamland.

KOLBY

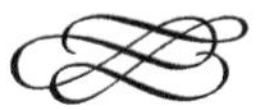

The next morning, I got up before Myla and made her breakfast. It's literally the only meal I knew how to make. Since Kamden hadn't left for work yet, I made enough for him, too. He came in the kitchen as I was finishing up and sat at our breakfast bar.

"Aye, you hooked me up?" he asked when he saw how much I'd made.

"Yeah, there's enough for you. Myla probably won't eat much, anyway. She gets full real quick.

"Thanks, bruh. Y'all been good since that whole Corette shit?"

"Yep."

"That's cool. When are you taking her to see the houses?"

"Shhh! Not so loud. I'm taking her today."

"My bad. I thought you told her about it."

"Naw, man. I'm trying to surprise her."

"Have you talked to her at all about moving to Chicago?"

"Not yet. Gonna do that today, too."

He looked at me and shook his head. "I hope it all works out for you, bruh."

He inhaled his breakfast and left for work. I went to my bedroom to check on Myla and she was coming out of the bathroom.

"I smell bacon," she said before kissing my lips.

"Yeah. I made breakfast and I was coming to see if you were awake. We need to leave here by ten."

I lifted her shirt and planted a kiss on her stomach.

"Good morning to my prince and princess. I hope you got some sleep after your busy day yesterday." I glared up at Myla before leaving a kiss on her navel.

"Get over it, baby. I had a good time bonding with your mother."

"Yeah, okay."

"I'm hungry. Is Kamden gone?"

"Yeah, he just left. Why?"

"So, I don't have to cover up."

I followed her out of the bedroom, looking at her ass cheeks peeking from underneath my T-shirt. My baby was getting thick in all the right places and I was loving that shit. She sat at our kitchen table instead of at the breakfast bar. After heating up her food in the microwave, I poured her a glass of orange juice, and took it to the table.

"Thank you, baby. Can you grab my prenatal vitamins? They're in the bathroom on the counter."

Without replying, I went to get her vitamins then came back and joined her at the table.

"You ate without me?" she pretended to be sad.

"I was hungry and I didn't know how long you'd be asleep."

"You're gonna sit here and watch me eat?"

"What's wrong with that? You're beautiful."

She smiled and looked down at her food. "Thank you. So, what does my handsome man have planned for today?"

"That's a surprise. You know, this is the longest stretch of time we've spent together. Are you sick of me, yet?"

"Not at all. I miss you while you're at work."

"I love coming home to you, which is something I want to talk to you about."

"I'm listening."

"You're about to reach the six-month mark, and we haven't talk about our living arrangements. Before you get too much further along, we need to decide how we're gonna do this."

"I agree. I've been waiting for you to bring it up."

"If my job had a location in Seattle, I would have already packed up my shit and transferred."

"But they don't, and you want me to move to Chicago."

"I don't just want, I *need* you to move to Chicago, as soon as possible."

"As soon as possible? There's a lot to be done to get ready for such a big move. And are we ready to take this next step? We haven't been—"

"Let's not go there, Myla. We got two whole-ass babies coming in three months, or less. Regardless of how long we've been together, that shit ain't gon' change. I don't plan to be a long-distance man or father."

"I don't want you to be."

"Then what's the problem?"

"There isn't one. When do you want me to start moving?"

"Are you serious?"

"I am. I love you and I want the four of us to be together."

I almost knocked her plate from the table when I rushed to swoop her into my arms. I picked her up and twirled her around, careful not to put pressure on her stomach. When I put her down, our lips connected in a passionate kiss.

A COUPLE OF HOURS LATER, we were headed to look at the first of three houses. All three of the houses were in a suburb right outside of the city. I've never pictured raising a family in Chicago, although I don't want to be too far away, because I do love my city. Not to mention, Myla is not a big-city girl and I want her to be comfortable.

"The babies want to know where we're going," Myla said.

"The babies gotta wait and see, just like their mama."

She folded her arms across her chest and pouted. It was cute how her arms rested on her belly.

With a chuckle, I said, "We'll be there in five minutes."

She clapped her hands and cheered, making me laugh again.

When we pulled up to the first house, I parked behind my realtor's car. He got out when he saw us pull up.

"Stay here for a sec, baby," I told Myla as I got out.

"Wassup, man," Vic greeted, along with a handshake.

"Just ready to find a house for my family, bruh."

Vic and I graduated from Leo Catholic High School together. He's one of the few niggas that I kept in touch with from high school. Vic married his college sweetheart a few years ago and they have a one-year old daughter.

"Hell, you pushing thirty. It's about time you slow down."

"Ain't shit out here but trouble. Let me get my girl and we'll meet you inside."

I walked around to the passenger side and before I could get the door open good, Myla was asking questions.

"Who's that guy?"

"That's my boy, Vic. We went to high school together."

"Oh. Is this his house?"

"Baby, will you get out and stop asking questions?"

She took my hand and slowly exited the vehicle. We held hands as we approached the house. Vic left the door open, so we went right inside.

"Umm, baby, did he just move in? Why would he invite us over and he doesn't have furniture yet?"

"This ain't his house, My," I said, shaking my head at her silly ass.

Vic came from around the corner and immediately put his hand out to greet Myla.

"Hello, Myla. It's nice to finally meet you. I'm Vic Swanson."

"Nice to meet you, too," Myla replied with a look of confusion.

"Baby, Vic is our realtor. He's gonna show us a few houses today."

"Houses? Are you for real, baby?"

"You think I'm gonna move you and the babies into that apartment with Kam?"

"Well, no, but I just agreed to move a couple of hours ago. How did you know I would say yes?"

I shrugged my shoulders. "Wishful thinking?"

"You're lucky I love you. Vic, can you show us around?"

"Of course. Umm, did I hear you say, *babies*? Are you having twins?"

"Yeah and we haven't told the family so keep that on the low," I told him.

"Two for one, huh," Vic said with a grin. "Congratulations!"

"Thanks, bruh."

Vic took us on a tour and Myla seemed to like everything about the house. There were four bedrooms, two-and-a-half bathrooms, a formal living room, a family room, a dining room, a large eat-in kitchen, and a basement that was large enough to create some office space.

Myla liked the other two houses that we saw, as well. I left the final decision up to her but I think she's leaning toward the first house. Before we went home, we stopped and had a late lunch. By the time we got back to my apartment, Myla was struggling to keep her eyes open.

"Let's wait until tomorrow to tell them about the babies. I don't feel like company tonight. I just wanna lay up under you and rub on you."

We'd just gotten in and were headed straight to the bedroom.

"We can't cancel, now. They've probably already made plans to be here."

"About that...I forgot to send the text."

"Kolbyyyy, you didn't send the text?"

"My bad, baby. It kind of slipped my mind. It was an exciting morning. I have an idea, though."

MYLA

Kolby's idea was for us to record a video announcing the twins and my move to Chicago, and then send a group text. So, after we took a nap, we got ready to record the video.

I put my hair up in a bun and a applied a light beat on my face. I figured once our family saw the video, we could post it to our social media accounts. I wanted to be cute. We decided to wear plain white T-shirts and blue jeans. Kolby wrote *girl* on one side of my stomach and *boy* on the other with a *Wite-Out* pen. He brought a stool from the breakfast bar to his bedroom and got his phone ready to record. Once I was situated on the stool, he pressed the red button and came to stand behind me.

"Hello family! I'm sure you're wondering why we sent this video," I said.

"We thought this would be the easiest way to tell you some exciting news," Kolby added.

"As you know, Kolby and I are starting a family." I rubbed my belly. "Today, he asked me to move to Chicago and I agreed."

"Not only did she agree, she also chose our new home, and we will be signing the paperwork within the next few weeks."

"We also have one more thing to tell you. Last month, we told you that we didn't find out the baby's gender. Well...we lied."

"We're finally ready to share with you what we found out," Kolby said.

Then together, we both shouted, "We're having...," Kolby put his hands on top of mine, and we both lifted my T-shirt. "A boy and a girl!" we said, excitedly.

I tilted my face back toward Kolby. He bent down to kiss my lips, then leaned down a bit more to kiss my stomach.

"That's right, Prince and Princess Ross will be here some time in February. Thanks for tuning in!" Kolby added before going to turn off the video.

"They're about kill us!" I said.

"Yup!"

He sat next to me on the bed and we watched the video, getting a good laugh at ourselves. It was corny, but still very cute. He trimmed the video at the beginning and end to make sure it started and stopped in the right places, then sent it to me, along with everyone of importance in our lives. We sat quietly for a few minutes, in our thoughts.

"Who do you think is gonna curse us out first?" I asked.

"Kolbbbyy!!!" we heard from the living room.

"I guess we got our answer," he said with a chuckle.

Kamden didn't even knock on the door. He barged in holding his phone in the air.

"Twins, bruh? *Twins!*" he shouted.

"That's what we said."

"I can't believe y'all kept this a secret for damn near a month. That's messed up. I'm your brother. We share the same DNA and you didn't even tell me."

"We didn't tell anybody. Mama found out accidently last week, and Myla told her mom yesterday."

Suddenly, both me and Kolby's phones rang.

"Oh shit!" he said as we gave each other a look.

Braelynn was calling me and Kyree was calling Kolby. He left the bedroom to take the call as I answered my phone.

"Helloooo," I sang.

"Are you fa real, sis? My so-called best friend since seventh grade. Have you really known for weeks that you were having my niece *and* nephew and you ain't say shit? I think it's time I reevaluate our friendship."

"Brae, it wasn't like that. We just wanted to surprise ya'll. So...surprise!"

"But we're best friends. I—"

"Oh, I gotta go. Jaelynn is calling."

I ended the call with Braelynn, then connected Jaelynn, answering with the same, "Helloooo."

"Don't damn helloooo me! Twins, My. And you ain't say shit. You tell us in a group text. I thought we were better than that."

"Jae, don't be like that. I love all y'all but this was something that Kolby and I decided. We wanted to keep it to ourselves for a little while."

I heard her exhale. "I guess y'all are entitled to that. Well, congratulations. Are you excited?"

"Honestly, Jae, I wasn't a first. It took me a couple of days to process, then I was good. Shit, I gotta go. My brother's FaceTiming me."

"Don't curse me out, Myles," I said as soon as we connected.

"I'm in shock. You know I'm already having a hard time with you being pregnant. This shit is too much, baby sis. And you moving to Chicago to be with that nigga. My baby is having two babies. This shit wild!"

With Myles and I being six years apart, he'd always acted like he was my daddy. He took his job as the protective big brother seriously, but he was never overbearing. I can imagine this being a lot for him to deal with. His voice cracked a bit as he spoke and he was teary-eyed.

"I know. But I'm still your baby sister. You know you're the best big brother ever, and I wouldn't be who I am today without your love and guidance."

"Naw, I ain't do shit but try to guide you away from niggas like me. At first it didn't work, but I think you got it right this time; and tell that nigga he bet' not fuck up. I'm proud of you My-My and I'm gon' make your ass proud of me, too. Let me get off this phone before you see me crying like a bitch. I love you."

I laughed as I wiped tears from my eyes. "I love you, too."

We disconnected and I sat there for a minute trying to get myself together. Thankfully, I didn't get any more calls. I'd sent my mother a text earlier about my decision to move and she already knew about the babies, so I didn't expect her to call.

Kolby was ending a FaceTime call with his parents when I entered the living room. Kamden sat on the couch, looking as if he was still in disbelief. When he saw me, a smile graced his lips.

"Damn, sis! You got my niece *and* nephew in there."

"That's what we were told."

"I ain't even a sappy nigga; but can I touch your stomach? This shit is amazing to me," he confessed.

"Don't you think you should be asking *me* if you can rub all on my woman and kids?" Kolby interjected.

"Baby, don't be like that."

I went and sat next to Kamden. His eyes were as big as a kid in a candy store, already. Then, suddenly, my stomach moved.

"Oh shit! What the hell?" Kamden said with surprise, yanking his hand back.

"Baby, come here. The babies are moving," I yelled to Kolby.

He ran over to the couch and sat on the other side of me. I took his hand and put it where I felt the babies move. This was the first time that the babies had moved and their movements could be seen, and felt on the outside of my stomach. I'd been feeling flutters for a while. Kamden watched in awe as my stomach started to move again. Kolby was in shock.

"Daammnnn! That look too crazy. You got two whole human beings in there," Kamden said.

He lifted his phone, I assumed, to record or take pictures. Kolby still hadn't said a word and when I looked at him, a single tear trickled from his eye.

"Aww, baby!" I said, comforting him with a kiss on his cheek.

"Aww, hell! Let me give y'all some privacy," Kamden said, leaving us on the couch.

"Thank you, baby."

"Why are you thanking me?"

"Because you didn't have to do this. You had other options and you chose to keep my seeds, not knowing what would happen between us."

He wrapped his arms around my body and gently rested his head on my stomach.

"Oh, baby," was all I could manage to say as I began to cry.

A knock on the door gained our attention. Kamden went to answer it and returned with his parents, Kyree, and Braelynn. They came with a big pot of beef stew and cornbread that Ms. Stella made. For the next few hours, we talked about the babies and my big move. Kolby didn't get to lay up under me like he planned, but the smile couldn't be wiped from his face. I didn't know if I'd ever seen him so happy. Today was a great day!

KOLBY

Once Myla and I posted the video of our announcement on our Facebook and Instagram pages, it gained over a million views overnight. Two of Chicago's most popular radio stations and two of Seattle's, contacted us for an interview. It wasn't that big of a deal because all we had to do was call in, but it was pretty cool. We shared our love story and they all gave us gift cards to use for baby items.

A moving company also reached out to us and offered to move Myla's stuff from Seattle for free. *Windy City Live,* a Chicago morning talk show that is recorded with a live studio audience, also contacted us and we are scheduled to appear on the show in a few weeks. It was an exciting time.

To add to the excitement, Kyree had the grand opening for his auto shop. Or should I say him and Braelynn's auto shop... and it was a huge success. He surprised Braelynn by naming it *K and B's Auto Shop* and adding her to all of the paperwork, making it legitimately owned by both of them. Braelynn's family was there to show their support and everyone got along well. I'm sure they were both still on cloud nine.

Myla and I flew back to Seattle on Sunday so that we could make it to our doctor's appointment scheduled for the next morning. Everything with the babies was on track and going as expected. Myla now had to visit the doctor every two weeks.

When we told Dr. Mavers that Myla would be moving to Chicago before the babies were born, she almost cried, which caused Myla to get emotional, as well. However, Dr. Mavers' college roommate had her own practice in Chicago and she connected us with her office. Dr. Mavers shared with us that Myla might only have one more visit with her, depending on how quickly we could get her packed and ready to go.

It was Monday evening and Myla and I had been lounging around since we got back from the doctor. My flight back to Chicago was tomorrow night and I already knew that it would be hard leaving her.

I watched her as she tapped away on her laptop. While in Chicago, she didn't do a lot of work for *MyLynn's Bedroom Boutique*. Her main role in the business that she owned with Braelynn and Jaelynn, was maintaining and updating their website with new items, which is what she'd been doing for the last two hours.

"I miss you, baby."

"What? I'm right here," she replied without looking up from her laptop.

"I know. You've been right there for two hours. I'm bored."

She looked up from her screen. "Did I bother you when you were working?"

"But I'm leaving tomorrow."

She rolled her eyes and shook her head. "Give me twenty more minutes. I'm almost done."

"I'm starting my timer. You probably don't know how to tell time."

She threw one of her throw pillows at me and I caught it before it hit me in the head. I was serious, though, and started the timer on my phone. While I waited, I checked my social media accounts.

We both had to turn off our notifications because it became a tad overwhelming when the video went viral. When I opened the Facebook app, I had four hundred notifications of which I had no intention of checking.

Over on Instagram, it was much of the same. Hundreds of notifications and follows. I debated on whether or not I should make my account private but ended up deciding against it. This would all die down soon, I was sure. I checked my DM's on Instagram and there weren't very many, thankfully. But there was one from Corette that was sent yesterday. I can't lie, I was tempted to see what she had to say but instead, I blocked her from viewing my account. I didn't need those types of problems in my life.

The alarm sounded and I turned it off, then looked at Myla. She was so into her work that she didn't even hear it. I got up from the couch and stood in front of the sofa chair that she was sitting in. When she didn't notice me, I reached for her laptop.

"Baby, what are you going?" she whined.

"Is your work saved?"

"Yes, it's saved. But I need like, five more minutes."

"No, the fuck you don't."

I took the laptop and put it on the end table next to the sofa chair. Then I took one of her hands and put it on my dick.

"Do you feel this shit? I've been sitting over there about to get blue balls."

She pulled her hand away and smacked her lips. "Boy, stop playing. We've literally had sex every day; except maybe once or twice over the last two and a half weeks. There is no way you about to get no damn blue balls."

I took both of her hands and pulled her up. When she was steady on her feet, I lifted her chin and leaned down to kiss her lips. When our tongues met, she let a moan slip and I almost lifted her by the ass and wrapped her legs around my waist, but her stomach prohibited that. My dick rubbed against her stomach while we kissed, and I began to slow-walk her toward the couch.

"Just let me get this nut and I'll go make you some breakfast food for dinner," I told her when our mouths disconnected. "I'll be quick and you can work while I cook."

"Nigga, I don't want breakfast for dinner, and ain't nothing ever quick about sex with you."

"Baby, this pussy gets juicier and juicier every day and I'm gon' be a thirty second brotha in a minute. Take them shorts off, then turn around and put your knees on the couch."

"Oh, you about to hit it from the back."

She smiled and began to wiggle out of her shorts. Since her stomach had gotten bigger, that was her favorite position. I began to ease out of my shorts and her doorbell rang. She looked at me like this was my damn place.

"Who you expecting?" I whispered.

"Nobody. And Mommy and Myles know you're here so they would call first."

The doorbell sounded again and Myla started pulling her shorts up.

"Naw, don't put those shorts back on. Ignore that shit. Baby! Come back over here. Shit!"

I watched her look out of the peephole and step back suddenly. Her actions caused me to go see who was on the other side of the door. Whoever it was, I didn't recognize, so I turned to look at Myla for answers.

"Who is that? Why do you look like you've seen a ghost?"

"It's Chase!"

"Myla, I can hear you. Open the door!"

"Who the fuck is Chase?"

"He's...he's my ex. How does he know where I live?"

I opened the door and came face-to-face with this nigga, so I could find out the purpose of his visit.

"Wassup?"

"I need to speak to Myla."

"The fuck you want with my girl, nigga?"

He released an angry chuckle. "Your girl, huh?"

I stepped outside and got right in the nigga's face. "That's what the fuck I said."

"Baby, please," Myla said, from behind me.

I could tell the moment that Myla came into his view. The nigga had the nerve to lick his lips and grab his dick.

"Damn, My," he said. "My seeds got you looking damn good."

The fuck? My fist met his jaw with a right hook. He stumbled off the one step in front of her door but didn't fall. I felt Myla's hand on my shoulder and heard her urging me to come back inside. As she pulled me, I stepped back, keeping my eyes on him. His hand went to his mouth and he spat out blood before he spoke.

"Myla didn't tell you about me?"

"Why would I?" she said from behind me.

"How we hooked up for old time's sake."

My eyes went back and forth between the two of them. My mind started replaying the past three months and questioning everything. *Was it all a lie?*

"Nigga, I wouldn't fuck you if you were the last man on earth. I haven't seen you in years."

"Tell this nigga the truth and send his ass back to Chicago. We got a family to raise."

I tried to go after him again but Myla had a grip on me and I didn't want to hurt her in the process of trying to get to him. I thought about the first three months of her pregnancy, when I had no idea that she was pregnant. *Was she afraid to tell me because she didn't know who the father was? Has she been playing me this whole fucking time?*

"Myla, what the fuck is this nigga sayin'?"

"Baby, I haven't seen or talked to him in years," she said to me, then looked at Chase. "Why the fuck would you come over her lying, Chase? Haven't you hurt me enough?"

She released the grip that she had on me and charged toward

him, swing her arms, and clocked him in the face. I pulled her back and took her back inside, closing the door behind me.

"It's just a matter of time, Myla. The truth will come out," Chase shouted through the door.

"Shut your bitch-ass up! I hate you, Chase," she screamed as she banged on the door.

I pulled her away from the door and took her to the couch, making her sit down. She hugged herself, arms resting on her stomach, as she rocked back and forth. The tears ran furiously down her face as she mumbled angrily. I hated seeing her like this but I had some questions.

"When was the last time you slept with him?"

She stopped rocking and looked up at me. Even in her current state, nose running, face wet with tears, eyes red, she was beautiful.

"What do you mean?"

"I mean exactly what the fuck I said, My. When was the last time you fucked him?"

She tilted her to the side and her eyebrows met in the middle as she frowned.

"Are you for real right now?"

"It's a simple question with a simple answer."

Slowly standing from the couch, she put her hand on her stomach and walked away. I followed her to the bedroom.

"Just tell me if there's a possib—"

She turned around and slapped the taste out of my mouth.

"I told you in Belize that I hadn't had sex in three years. That was the last time I had sex with him. Now...I want you to get your shit and get the fuck out. You can take your ass back to Chicago and don't bother coming back!"

While I stood there holding my cheek, she went in the bathroom and threw my toiletries in my travel bag, tossed it out the door, then slammed it shut. I stood there, feeling like the dumbest muthafucka on earth. *Why did I let this nigga knock me off my square?* Going to the bathroom door, I could hear her sniffling on the other side.

"Baby, I fucked up. I'm sorry."

"Yeah, you are sorry. Now take your sorry ass on up outta here."

"Please, let's just talk this through. I don't want to leave."

"But you wanna believe that I'm around here lying on my pussy. Kolby, I need you to go. I need some time and I don't want to see your fuckin' face right now. Please."

"I'll give you a couple of hours but when I come back, we need to talk."

"Just go!" she shouted through the door.

I stood there debating whether or not I should leave. Finally, I grabbed a hoodie, and the keys to the rental and left, with no place to go.

[illegible] in the [illegible] anything on [illegible]

[illegible]

[illegible] up outta here."

[illegible] wait to leave [illegible]

[illegible] here [illegible] on [illegible]

[illegible] time and I don't want to [illegible]

[illegible] you a couple of hours ago when I came back [illegible]

[illegible] shouted through the door.

I stood there debating whether or not I should leave [illegible]

[illegible]

MYLA

My heart was broken...shattered into a million pieces. I stayed in the bathroom for a while after I heard Kolby leave. I couldn't believe he actually believed a word that came out of Chase's mouth and questioned me about the shit. That fucked me up.

I sat on my bed and unplugged my phone from the charger, then went to Jaelynn's contact. As I waited for her to pick up, my hands began to shake, my lips began to quiver, and my breathing became shallow. Tears fell from my eyes uncontrollably.

"Hey, My!" Jaelynn answered.

I tried to speak but I was too choked up.

"Hello? My, are you there?"

I released a scream that was so loud, I was sure that my entire block probably heard me.

"Are you home? I'm on my way. Don't hang up."

My phone fell to the floor as I wrapped my arms around my body to try comforting myself. I had never felt a pain so deep, not even when Chase broke up with me. I fell on my back and rolled to my side, then pulled my knees up as far as I could. My cries of agony didn't cease as Jaelynn recited comforting words on her way to me.

"I'm outside, My. I'll let myself in," I heard her say.

Minutes later, she came inside my bedroom and crawled onto the bed with me. She pulled my head onto her lap and rubbed my back.

"My, please, tell me what's wrong. Where's Kolby? I thought he didn't leave until tomorrow."

Just the mention Kolby's name sent me into another fit of tears. After ten minutes of sobbing, I got myself together enough to tell her what happened. Jaelynn was pissed at both Kolby and Chase by the time I was done.

"I'm calling Myles. He gon' fuck Chase up."

I met Chase through Myles because they were cool. Myles didn't want me to date Chase but I didn't listen. When Chase got tired of sneaking around, he asked for Myles' blessing to date me. He didn't want to, but he gave us his blessing, anyway. Of course, their friendship ended when Chase broke my heart. They still ran in the same circle but they weren't cool, not even a little bit. I made Myles promise not to do anything to Chase when we broke up and he's kept his word. I was sure that wouldn't be the case once Myles heard what had happened.

Before Jaelynn could call Myles, my phone rang. She picked it up from the floor and answered, then put it on speaker.

"Hey, Brae."

"What the fuck is going on? Kolby called Kyree talking in circles about Chase, Myla, and the babies."

"It's a whole-ass mess and Chase gon' get beat the fuck down for this fuck shit."

"Tell me what happened."

Jaelynn began to tell Braelynn what happened and suddenly there was some banging on the door.

"Hold on, Brae. My, stay here."

Before she made it to the door, I heard my brother's voice.

"Myla, tell me you ain't backtrack and fuck that nigga," Myles yelled when he entered my bedroom.

"Brae, I'll call you back."

"No, wait!" Braelynn yelled before the call ended.

"You know what? Fuck you and Kolby's dumb ass for even questioning me about this bullshit."

"My-My, I had to ask. Glenn said the nigga been going around telling anybody who would listen that the twins was his."

"Don't fucking talk to me Myles. Get the fuck out!"

Jaelynn pulled him out of my bedroom and said something to him that I couldn't hear. About five minutes later, she returned and sat next to me on my bed, then pulled me into a hug.

"I'm so sorry this is happening, sis. Myles gon' beat Chase's ass for you."

"Fuck him and Kolby, acting like I don't know who the fuck fathered my kids."

Then came more tears. This time, they were tears of anger. Angry at Chase for being such a sorry-ass nigga to stir up all this bullshit. Angry at Kolby for not loving me enough to see past the lies spewing from Chase's mouth. Angry at Myles for not thinking enough of me to know that I wouldn't fuck Chase after the way he broke my heart.

My body began to tremble again, and I felt lightheaded and nauseous. When I looked at Jaelynn, my vision was blurred. I could vaguely see her mouth moving. It looked to be in slow motion and she sounded muffled.

"Myla! Myla! Can you hear me?"

I felt her arms around me as she guided me to my bed. Then, everything went black.

KOLBY

W*hat the fuck was I thinking? Why did I ask her that? I should have stayed and made her talk to me. I fucked up.* The realization at how badly I fucked up hit me hard. It was like, my heart knew the nigga was lying, but my ego was saying, "Just ask her nigga, so you can be sure."

The hurt that flashed across her face before she became angry should have shut me the fuck up. The slap across the face brought me back to my senses, though. *Why am I so stupid?*

I left Myla's house in a fucked-up headspace, having no idea where I was going. After driving around aimlessly for about thirty minutes, I came across a twenty-four-hour breakfast spot and decided to check it out. Inside, I was seated quickly. As I looked over the menu, a waitress approached the table.

"Hello, handsome. I'm Ms. Marianne, and I'll be your server this evening. Can I get you something to drink?"

"I'll just have a glass of water. Thank you."

"Are you ready to order your meal?"

"Umm, not really. I don't even have an appetite. I'm not sure why I'm here."

I put the menu down and rubbed my hand down my face. When I looked up again, Ms. Marianne was sitting across from me.

"You look very familiar. Have you been here before?"

"No ma'am."

"Hmm. Well, I can tell something is bothering you. I could feel it all in your spirit when I approached you. Do you want to talk about it?"

Ms. Marianne was an older, Black woman, probably in her late fifties. She seemed very motherly, but I didn't know her like that, to be telling her all my business.

"I promise, I'm not some kind of weird old lady," she assured me when I hesitated. "I'll have the cook make you one of my favorites and when I come back, you can tell me what has you feeling down."

She left before I agreed, leaving me to my thoughts. I looked at my phone and had several text messages from Kyree. I'd called him on an angry rant when I left Myla's place. I hung up on him, so he's probably still trying to figure out what's going on. Ignoring his messages, I put my phone away and waited for my food.

When Ms. Marianne returned, she had a plate with three large pancakes, another with scrambled eggs and bacon, and a bowl with cheesy grits. I looked at the food, then back at her in amazement. The appetite that was nonexistent, suddenly reappeared.

"Wow! Thank you. This all looks great."

"You're welcome, handsome. You go ahead and dig in. I'm gonna grab you a glass of orange juice. When I come back, we're gonna figure out how to fix your problem."

I said my grace and prepped my food, putting some butter on the fluffy pancakes, before cutting them up and drowning them in syrup. After adding some salt and pepper to my eggs and grits, I dug in. Ms. Marianne came back with a tall glass of orange juice and slid into the booth.

"How is everything?"

"It's delicious," I replied after chewing and swallowing a bite.

"Well, whenever you're ready, start talking."

You would have thought I'd be uncomfortable with this woman that I didn't know from Adam, sitting across from me, watching me eat, but I wasn't. Instead, she had a very calming aura about her. After enjoying a few more bites, I began.

"I messed up with my lady and the mother of my children," I confessed.

"Are these one in the same?"

"Huh?" I questioned, momentarily confused. "Oh, yes. It's the same woman."

"What happened?"

"Ms. Marianne, it's a long story. You want me to start from the beginning."

She looked around the almost empty restaurant before saying, "I ain't got nothing but time."

While I enjoyed the best breakfast food I've ever had, I shared the story of how I fell in love with Myla Rae Abbott. By the time I got to how I ended up in the restaurant, drowning my sorrows in pancakes, I felt like a complete asshole. I didn't need Ms. Marianne to tell me that I was wrong, I knew that shit as soon as I felt the sting of Myla's hand across my face. I needed to know how to fix it, so I asked her exactly that.

"How am I gonna fix the mess I've made?"

"Do you love her?"

"I love her and I'm in love with her."

"Do you truly believe that she hasn't slept with her ex and those babies are yours?"

"With everything in me."

"Then why would you allow her ex to make you doubt what you already know as fact?"

"Ms. Marianne, I don't know. I could tell from his demeanor when I opened the door that he was there to start some bull. Now that I think about it, he probably saw the video of Myla and I that went viral when we announced that we were having twins."

"That's it!" she almost shouted as she clapped her hands together. "That's where I've seen your face. She's from here in Seattle, right."

"Yes, ma'am."

"My daughter showed it to me because I don't have all that social media stuff. We both thought it was adorable; the love between you two just oozed through the phone screen."

"Thank you. I've never felt about anyone the way I feel about Myla. Falling in love with her was the easiest thing I've ever done and I have no doubt that she feels the same way about me."

"Her ex got jealous and realized that he lost a good thing. Instead of being mature about it and wishing her well, he tried to ruin it...and you fell for it."

I looked down at my empty plate and shook my head.

"Yeah...hook, line, and sinker. I need to go apologize."

"Oh, you're gonna need to do more than apologize, young man. First, you need to acknowledge your fears."

"Fears?"

"Yes, fears. Everyone is afraid of something? What are you afraid of, son?"

I was with everything Ms. Marianne was saying up until that point.

"Umm, I'm not—"

"Don't tell that lie," she said while shaking her head. "Think about it before you start denying it. Six months ago, you were enjoying the single life, not looking to settle down, dating multiple women, I'm sure. You are now responsible for three other people. She's uprooting her whole life, expecting you to take care of her and the babies you created. And you're gonna sit there and tell me you don't have any fears? I call bullshit!"

Well, damn! Who is this woman? Is she some kind of mind reader?

"Talk to me, son."

"You're right! Things changed quickly and I can't say that I was prepared. Knowing that I'm responsible for three lives is scary as hell. Even still...I wouldn't change a thing. I want it all and I'll do whatever I have to do to have them in my life."

"Your apology needs to come from the heart and she has to believe that your words are genuine. You need to admit that you were wrong and be prepared to tell her why you were wrong. You think you can do that?"

"Yes, ma'am."

"Then what are you still sitting here for? Go get your woman back."

I stood and took my debit card from the little compartment on my phone case. When I handed it to Ms. Marianne, she said, "This one's on me. Now, go!"

Surprising myself, I wrapped her in a hug and kissed her cheek before saying, "Thank you!"

I rushed to my car, hopped in, and took off, headed toward Myla's. When I got to a stoplight, my phone rang and I dug it out of the front pocket of my hoodie. It was Myla.

"Baby, I'm so—"

"This is Jaelynn. Meet me at the UW Medical Center ER. Myla passed out."

"What! Shit! I'm on my way!"

The light had changed to green but I didn't give a fuck. I didn't move until I pulled up the address of the hospital. Praying the entire way, I broke the speed limit trying to get to my baby.

MYLA

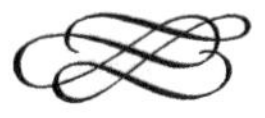

I opened my eyes and looked around at the white walls. Machines were beeping and it smelled like a hospital, letting me know exactly where I was. I couldn't quite recall the events that led to me being here, but hands immediately went to my stomach and relief washed over me when I realized that nothing happened to my babies.

"Baby!"

"Myla!"

Kolby had been sitting next to the bed with his head resting on my leg. Jaelynn was sitting in a chair not too far from the bed. They both were in my face as soon as they realized I was awake. Before I could respond, my mother and brother rushed in.

"My baby!" my mom said.

"You good, My-My?" Myles asked.

They all stood around the bed with worried looks on their faces.

"I feel fine. What happened?"

"You got really upset and passed out. When we got here, your blood pressure was very high. The ER doctor thinks that's what made you pass out."

As she spoke, it all began to come back to me. Chase coming to my house spewing lies. Kolby questioning me about the shit Chase said. Myles coming over questioning me as well. Suddenly, the machine began to beep and seconds later, a nurse rushed in.

"I need you all to step out, please."

"I'm not leaving," Kolby said calmly.

"Sir, it's very—"

"I'm not leaving!" he repeated, not nearly as calmly as before.

"He can stay," I told the nurse.

I was pissed at him, but I was sure he was worried about the babies.

Everyone else left and the nurse did whatever she needed to do, checking all the machines.

"Looks like the babies are doing fine but your blood pressure began to increase very quickly. Whatever is causing stress or upsetting you, needs to be avoided. Dr. Mavers is here and will be in shortly to check on you and let you know if she wants to keep you overnight. Make sure you stay relaxed."

"Thank you," I said as she left.

Not even ten seconds later, the door opened and Kolby turned around and said, "Can we have a few minutes alone, please?"

I didn't see who it was but I'm assuming one of the three that had just left. Kolby never left my side, not even when the nurse was checking me out. The bed was in a slightly raised positioned so that I was sitting up. He leaned in and kissed my forehead before he returned to the chair that was next to the bed.

Taking my hand his, he kissed the back of it, then placed his free hand on my stomach. Unintentionally, my body tensed, but I looked away from him on purpose.

"Baby, I fucked up...I fucked up, I was wrong and I'm sorry. I let that nigga get in my head when I know in my heart that none of that shit he was saying is true. There hasn't been a moment that I've ever doubted that these are my babies. I love you and I can't lose you because I'm a dumbass."

Yes! You are a dumbass! I kept my head turned away from him as he spoke. He sounded sincere, and I'm sure he was, but my fucking feelings were hurt and wasn't forgiving his ass that easily.

"Look at me, baby." I ignored him. "I know I hurt you and it's killing me inside. My actions are the reason you're here and I'll never forgive myself for upsetting you so much that it put you and the babies in danger. I couldn't live with myself if something happened to you or our babies."

I refused look at him. He continued to hold my hand, giving it a little squeeze. His other hand remained on my stomach and he rubbed his hand over it. I felt him rest his head on the bed, near my hip. I still refused to look in his direction...until I heard him sniffle.

"You're my family now, baby. I don't want to lose you before I've had a chance to show you how much I love you. Just give me a chance to prove my love to you," he cried. *He's literally crying.*

"I forgive you," I whispered.

His head popped up and it broke my heart to see his face wet with tears. *How can I not forgive him? This man has my whole heart.*

"You forgive me?"

"I do...this time. But if you ever take someone else's word over mine again, I'm fucking you up."

He stood and placed a soft kiss on my lips. When he pulled away, his face hovered over mine and I lifted my hands to wipe his face. I then cupped his cheeks and kissed him again.

"I love you, Kolby, but you hurt my feelings."

"I know—"

"Let me finish. I know that sometimes we act off emotion and we say shit without thinking. I'm going to ask this one time, and then I don't want to talk about it anymore."

"Okay."

"Do you believe these babies are yours?"

"I have no doubts," he responded without hesitation, then sealed it with a kiss.

"Okay, lovebirds, break it up," Dr. Mavers said, scaring the shit out of us. "I'm guessing you're feeling okay?"

"I feel better. I never felt bad. I was dealing with a situation and got really angry, but I'm calm now."

As she listened, she looked through my chart and checked the numbers on the machines.

"This isn't the first time during this pregnancy that your blood pressure has been elevated. You need to be careful and stay away from things that trigger stress, I don't care what or who it is. I'm going to keep you overnight for observation just as a precaution and to monitor your blood pressure."

"Okay."

"You've been awfully quiet, Dad. No need to worry, she's fine, the babies are fine, this is just as a precaution," she assured Kolby.

"Can I stay with her?" he asked.

"As long as you're not the one stressing her out, of course. From what I saw when I walked in, I would say you're not the culprit," she said with a smile before continuing. "I'll have them get you set up in a room. It should only be about thirty minutes."

As she left, my mother, brother, and Jaelynn came in.

"Everything good?" Ma asked as she walked around to the other side of the bed to kiss my cheek.

"Yes, Mommy. Dr. Mavers wants to keep me for observation as a precaution."

"You straight My-My?" Myles asked.

"I'm fine, Myles," I said with an attitude and an eye-roll.

"You scared the sh—mess outta me, My," Jaelynn finally spoke up and gave me a hug. "Don't you ever do that again."

I laughed. "I'll try not to. I'm just glad you were there. Thank you, sis."

"Can I talk to my baby sister alone for a sec, y'all?"

"When y'all are done talking, we're gonna head out. Call me in the morning," Mommy said, then gave me another kiss on my cheek. "Love you, sweetheart."

"Love you, too, Mommy."

Jaelynn gave me a hug. "We'll talk more tomorrow when you're released. I'll call Brae and give her an update. Kolby, you may want to call your mom, too."

"I left my phone in the car. I'll go get it while y'all talk." He kissed my lips before he followed my mom and Jaelynn out.

"Say what you need to say, Myles."

"Don't be like that My-My. You know you mean more to me than anybody. I wanted to kill Chase ass for even having your name come out his mouth, but I needed to come see you first, to know that his death would be justified."

I finally looked at Myles...I mean, really looked at him. He had a cut on his lip, his eye was slightly swollen, and the skin on his knuckles was cut, as well.

"What did you do, Myles? You didn't—"

"Naw, I didn't kill 'em. Glenn and Dre was there and stopped me."

"Good."

"Listen, My-My, I'm sorry, okay. Before you got with ole boy, I always thought you had a weak spot for Chase. I know you loved that nigga like crazy at one point. I was happy as fuck you weren't pregnant by that nigga."

"I can't believe you even let the thought cross your mind. I've been over him for a long-ass time, Myles."

"I know, but everyone has weak moments, sis. I thought you may have slipped up. My bad, okay. I'm sorry. I can't have my heart mad at me."

I didn't even know why I was fooling myself. I'd never been able to stay mad at my brother for long. This time was no different. If I could forgive Kolby, I could forgive him.

"Okay."

"Okay, what?"

"Okay, I forgive you, but I'm gonna need you to stay away from me for a few days because I'm still mad."

"I'll give you twenty-four hours, but you better answer the phone when I call after that." He kissed my forehead.

"I said a few days."

"I heard you. I love you," he said on his way out.

"Love you, too."

KOLBY

Myla was released from the hospital the next morning. I canceled my flight and decided that I'd stay with her until she was ready to come back to Chicago, permanently. Being an accountant had its perks and one of them was not needing other people to do my job. I could work remotely as often as I needed. Any meetings I had, could be conducted through video conferencing and any paperwork I needed that I didn't have could be emailed or faxed.

Although things between Myla and I were back to normal, we hadn't discussed her move to Chicago since she'd been released from the hospital. We needed to start packing her things and contact the moving company, as soon as possible. We'd just finished eating Chipotle for dinner and Myla was relaxing on the couch. I cleaned up the kitchen then went and sat with her, putting her feet in my lap.

"Baby, we need to talk about the move," I said as I rubbed her feet.

"What about it?"

"The mortgage was approved, the inspection is early next week, and we should be able to move in within two to three weeks. We need to start packing."

"Okay. My lease isn't up until April. Myles is gonna stay here until then."

"Are you leaving the furniture for him?"

She shrugged her shoulders. "Do we need it or are we buying all new stuff? Can we even afford to furnish a whole house? Are the babies gonna share one nursery or will they each have their own? Do we—"

"Baby, calm down, please. You know what Dr. Mavers said."

I moved to the right and gently pulled her onto my lap as she began to cry. *Pregnant women cry an awful lot.*

"That's why I've been avoiding talking about the move. There's so much to do and we're trying to do everything so fast. Every day it's getting harder and harder for me to get shit done. How am I supposed to move halfway across the damn country? This is too much!" Her head rested on my shoulder as she cried.

"Listen, baby. Everything will work out, but I need you to be honest with me. Are you having doubts about moving? About us?"

She lifted her head and looked in my eyes. "Noo, noo, that's not it, baby. I want to move because I want to be with you. I want us to be a family. But I can't lie, this is all so overwhelming. Since the moment I found out I was pregnant, it's been...a lot. Not only was the pregnancy unplanned, then I find out I'm having not one, but two babies. I'm moving halfway across the country and I still have a third of a company to run and...it's just a lot. I don't know if I'm coming or going sometimes."

"Baby, believe it or not, I've thought about everything you just said. Six months ago, I was single and only responsible for myself. Now, I got three other people that I have to take care of. It's a lot and it can be overwhelming. Just know this...I wouldn't change a thing."

"You don't have any regrets?"

"The only regrets I have is not claiming you as mine before we left Belize and not being here for the first three months of the pregnancy. But look at how God hooked a nigga up. You mine now, so that's all that matters. I love you."

"I love you, too."

She adjusted her body so that she was straddling me. It was kind of awkward with her stomach as big as it was.

"What are you doing?" I asked her, although I knew.

"You've been holding out all week. I need some dick."

"Holding out? Who? Me? Never!"

"It's been almost a full week. You've been walking around here in sweats with no damn underwear, with your dick slanging all around."

"I was trying to be comfortable while I worked."

"No, your ass was teasing me. Are you gonna give me some dick or not? Because I do still have my vibrators. I almost used one the other day."

"No you didn't. I threw them bitches away last month," I told her with a satisfied smirk.

"Noooo! Why would you do that? Those things came in handy during my three-year sex hiatus. They were like... my best friends."

Her ass actually looked sad. If she wasn't pregnant, I might have tossed her ass across the room.

"Well, you got a new best friend now. Take that shit off and sit on your bestie."

THE TALK that Myla and I had was very necessary and so was the lovemaking that followed. The next day, I went to U-Haul and bought some boxes, then rounded up Ms. Delilah, Jaelynn, and Myles, so that they could help us start packing. For several afternoon or evenings, they came over with more boxes, dinner, and helping hands, for which we were grateful.

Myla's furniture was fairly new, so we decided that we'd keep it for the family room. We'd use her bedroom furniture for the master bedroom, since it was better than mine, and use my bedroom furniture for the fourth bedroom. The twins would share a room for the first couple of years and we'd use the third bedroom as a playroom.

We decided that just because we could move into our house in two to three weeks, we wouldn't rush this process. Thanksgiving was coming and Myla wanted to spend it in Seattle. I scheduled the movers for the Sunday after the holiday and Myla and I had a flight the following Monday morning. Things were falling into place perfectly.

MYLA

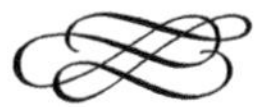

New Year's Eve

It'd been about five weeks since I officially moved to Chicago, or should I say LaGrange, a suburb that's about twenty minutes west. Aside from this deathly cold weather, I loved it. My favorite part of it all was being with Kyree every single day. We ended up choosing the first house that we looked at and I couldn't be happier.

We decided to decorate the nursey in green and yellow since the twins would be sharing. Since there would be no theme, we planned to add some décor that included their names or initials...as soon as they had names and initials. For whatever reason, we hadn't talked about names

I was very happy when Kolby agreed to spend Thanksgiving in Seattle with my family. I'm not sure how holidays will work in the future. My mom and Myles were supposed to come for Christmas, but their flight ended up getting canceled because of a damn snowstorm. I won't see them now until our baby shower.

A couple of days after we arrived back in Chicago, we had our appearance on *Windy City Live.* On the show, we shared our love story and talked about the babies. We credited Braelynn and Kyree with being the reason we met. Since they were in the audience, Val and Ryan, the hosts, ended up having them on the show with us, and they shared their love story as well.

We were able to promote, *MyLynn's Bedroom Boutique*, along with *K and B's Auto Shop*. Our sales have been off the chain since the airing and the auto shop has had an influx of customers, as well. On top of that, people on social media kept asking if they could send us monetary gifts for the twins. We ended up creating a CashApp for them under *$RossTwins* and people were constantly sending money.

I'm now at thirty-three weeks and praying I make it five more, even though I'm tired of being pregnant. Dr. Quincy, my new doctor that was recommended by Dr. Mavers, was just as great. At my last visit, she said that there was no reason to believe that I wouldn't carry them at least that long, but they would come when they were ready. So basically, be prepared.

Today's New Year's Eve and I refused to take my big ass outside in that ungodly weather. Kolby had been trying to plan something for a couple of weeks and I told him, straight up, that I wasn't leaving the house. After he made breakfast—the only meal he knows how to make—we sat down to eat. He told me he had some errands to run and that Braelynn would be coming over to help me get ready for our date.

"Kolby, I told you I didn't want to go anywhere. I'm too fat and it's freezing out there."

He pulled my chair between his legs. "Didn't I tell your fine ass to stop saying that shit. You ain't fat, baby. You're carrying two lives. Stop saying that shit. Okay?"

"Okay."

He kissed my lips and pushed my chair back to its original place.

"It's still too cold outside."

"We'll be inside, baby. I planned a date night in. The whole time we've been together, we've barely dated. Everything has been about the babies and moving you here."

I thought about what he said and he was right. We'd gone out to dinner here and there but we'd never gotten dressed up and gone to an event or had a night out on the town. But for some reason, I didn't feel like I'd missed anything. Just being with him was enough, we didn't have to be doing anything special.

"Aww, baby," I cooed as I slowly stood and moved to his lap. "Is that why you were pressing me so much? You don't feel like you courted me enough?"

"I didn't court you enough and I feel fucked up about it. Look at all you've done and sacrificed for me and I haven't even taken you out on a real date."

"Baby, just being with you is enough. I enjoy the time we spend together. I hadn't even noticed that we'd never been on a date until just now. All I need is you and I'm good."

He was really pouting and I put my finger under his chin and lifted his face, forcing him to look at me.

"We have our whole lives together, right?" He nodded. "Then we have time, right?" He nodded again and kissed my lips.

He put his hand on my stomach and spoke to the babies.

"I hope you two know how lucky you are to have her as your mama. You better treat her right when you get here, too."

He kissed my stomach and then lifted his head to kiss me again. I remained on his lap and he fed me from his plate, while he ate. When his was empty, he slid mine over and did the same. As we finished, the doorbell rang and while he cleaned up our dishes, I went to see who it was.

"Who is it?"

"Brae."

I opened the door and as soon as she saw me, she went to oohing and aahing over my belly.

"Oh my God, My! You look like you're about to pop."

"I am."

As I was about to close the door, I realized that Kyree was outside in the car.

"Is Kyree coming in?" I asked her.

"Nope. He said he was dropping me off, and not to ask him any questions."

I shrugged my shoulders, then closed and locked the door. Braelynn took off her shoes, then followed me to the kitchen.

"Y'all didn't save me no breakfast?"

"Kolby cooked. I didn't know you were coming until we sat down to eat."

"You can cook, Kolby? Your brother can't cook shit."

"All I can cook is a few breakfast foods," he told her.

"Kyree can't even do that. I tried to teach him a few simple meals and that shit went all the way wrong. He's literally banned from the kitchen," Braelynn said.

"Don't do my bro like that."

"It's true." She shrugged her shoulders. "Now, tell me what's up for today because my fiancé didn't tell me anything."

"Kyree and I wanted to give you both a day of pampering. Since Myla refuses to leave the house, we brought the pampering to you. By the time you leave here, Brae, you'll be ready for whatever Kyree has planned for tonight."

Braelynn and I looked at each, then back at Kolby before saying, "Okay."

KOLBY WAS GOING to get his soul sucked out of his dick tonight. The day that he and Kyree planned for us has been amazing, so far. Since he left, we've gotten a ninety-minute massage, I took a relaxing bath while Braelynn preferred a hot shower in our guest bathroom, and we'd just gotten our hair done. I don't know how they got all these people to come to us on New Year's Eve, but we were enjoying every minute of it.

After each professional performed their service, they told us what time the next person would arrive but didn't give us a clue as to what they were coming to do. While we waited, we chatted about any and everything.

"I think a makeup artist is coming next. Or maybe a stylist with some outfits because I don't have anything nice to wear that will fit."

"I guess we'll see in about twenty minutes," Braelynn said.

"I know I've been super distracted with my own life but you haven't said much about wedding plans. Have you started?"

"Sis, believe me, if I had started planning, you would be tired of me already. I wanted to have a short engagement but if I don't start planning something soon, it's gonna be longer than I want it to be. We've been so busy with the shop, plus I still have my third of *MyLynn's* to maintain. I've been swamped."

"That's a lot, Brae. I don't how I'm gonna manage with two infants at the same time. I'm so nervous."

"Now you know Ms. Stella been waiting on grandkids for years. I'm willing to bet she will retire early if you need her to."

We both laughed because it was absolutely true.

"I wouldn't allow her to do that. I'll be okay but I'm trying to mentally prepare myself for the challenge that I know this is gonna be. Kolby damn near works from home every day, so I know he'll be around to help a lot."

"You got all of us and I'm sure Auntie Dee will take some time off work as well. Jaelynn can work from anywhere and I know she's willing to come for as long as you need her."

"Speaking of Jae, what's up with her and Kam?" I asked. Those two had really been hush-hush about whatever they had going on.

"Nothing according to them. They're still claiming to just be good friends. He went to Seattle to hang with her tonight, though."

We looked at each other with raised eyebrows.

"For New Year's Eve? That's kinda..."

"Yeah. I know. I guess time will tell," she said.

We continued to chat and enjoy our day of pampering. The late afternoon continued, just as the early afternoon did. After having our make-up done by a professional MUA, a stylist came over with several beautiful gowns for us to choose from. It's been hard these past few months to feel beautiful, even with Kolby tells me every day, multiple times a day. However, after I'd chosen my gown and looked in the mirror, I couldn't deny how amazing I looked.

"Damn, sis! You killin' it, carrying twins and all."

"Thank you!" I replied as I turned to look at her. "Oh my God, Brae! You look amazing. Kyree gon' try to put a baby in you tonight, sis."

"Girl, his ass try that shit every night. I don't know how I'm not pregnant already."

"Are y'all still playing Russian roulette? I thought you were getting on the pill."

"I was but Kyree begged me not to. I don't really want to anyway and he still uses condoms...most of the time."

"You see this," I pointed to my stomach. "This gon' be yo' ass before the end of the year. Y'all keep playing."

We took some pictures to post later on social media. The dress she chose was emerald green and fit like a glove. It had a split on the side that went almost up to her damn waist. It was strapless and open in the back. Kyree would definitely have a hard time keeping his hands off her.

My dress was black and fitted as well, but the material was very comfortable and conformed to my curves. It had a boat neck, long sleeves, and a split that went up to the middle of my thigh, maybe a little higher.

"Are we supposed to call them and let them know we're ready or—"

"Daammn!"

"Shit!"

We heard near the door to the master bedroom, where Braelynn and I were. We turned around to see our men, two of the fine-ass Ross brothers, dressed like they'd just stepped out of *GQ* magazine.

KOLBY

Myla looked so fucking good. I was in complete awe of her beauty. All I could say was, "Daammn!"

I prayed she kept some of that baby weight, because that ass was sitting real nice.

"Why y'all sneaking up on us?" she fussed as I approached her. She looked so good I wanted to toss her on the bed and devour her.

"Baby, you look so beautiful. How do you feel? Did you enjoy everything?" I whispered with my forehead against hers and my hands on her stomach.

"Thank you, baby. I feel great. Today was everything. Thank you for making it so special."

I kissed her lips. "I would do anything to keep a smile on your beautiful face. I'm glad you enjoyed."

"Hey, lovebirds. We're about to head out," Kolby said. "I'm trying to put a baby up in this fine-ass woman tonight."

Braelynn and Myla gave each other a look and laughed. I raised an eyebrow at Kyree because he and I had just talked about that very topic. We all left the master bedroom and as I saw Kyree and Braelynn out, Myla headed toward the kitchen.

"Baby, you hired a chef?"

"How else were we gon' eat, baby? You know I'm not cooking."

She laughed. "Thank goodness. I guess I hadn't thought about it. When did the chef come in, though?"

"You ask too many questions. And stop trying to be nosy," I scolded her as she tried see what the chef was cooking. "Let's go in the dining room while we wait for his food to finish."

"Wait, baby. Can we have the chef take some pictures of us together first? I can't stay in these shoes much longer."

"Of course. Chef Lance, this is my lady, Myla. Would you mind taking a few pictures of us?"

"Nice to meet you, Ms. Myla. My pleasure."

We went to the formal living room. Aside from a few pictures on the walls, it was currently void of furniture. When we finished, Chef Lance handed me my phone and returned to the kitchen, while we went to the dining room. Myla was in front of me; she gasped when she saw the décor.

The table was decorated with a black tablecloth, and gold rose petals were scattered over the surface. There were only two place settings, one at the head and the other right next to it. The dishes were gold but trimmed in black. There was also a beautiful bouquet of black and gold roses on the table. Soft music played in the background from a portable speaker that I had connected to my iPad. I wrapped my arms around her from behind as she took everything in.

"Oh my God, baby. Did you do this yourself?"

"Of course not. Do you like it?"

"It's beautiful. Everything today has been perfect. Thank you."

"You deserve all of this and more. I wish I could give you the world."

I planted kisses on her neck and she leaned her head back to give me more access.

"You are my world, baby. You and the babies. I don't need anything else," she said, softly.

I turned her around to face me and as I began to speak, I got choked up. The love I felt for her was overwhelming at times, and I couldn't believe that she was mine and about to give birth to my children.

"I love you...so much, Myla," was all I could manage to say, although there was so much more I planned to say.

"I love you, too, baby. You okay?"

I nodded. "Let's sit down. The food should be ready soon."

I pulled out her chair and pushed her up as close as she could go. I sat at the head of the table and reached for the bottle of sparkling cider.

"You want some wine?" I asked, showing her the bottle.

"Boy, don't play. I thought I was about to have some wine for real. It's been way too long."

"Well, use your imagination, baby. No wine yet but this apple cider about to bang."

I poured us each a glass and put the bottle down.

"Let's toast," I suggested.

"To what?"

"I don't know. You do it."

"Okay." We looped our arms around each other's like people do when they're about to toast. "To unplanned pregnancy, unexpected twins, and undeniable love."

"I'll definitely drink to that." And we did. "Better than wine, right?"

"Umm, no, but it's good."

Chef Lance entered with our first course, which was an avocado caprese salad. He filled each of our plates and returned to the kitchen. I reached for both of Myla's hands and blessed the food. She took her first bite and moaned, causing me to look in her direction.

"What? This is so good."

"I thought I was the only one that could make you moan like that."

She looked at me and rolled her eyes before saying, "You and some good-ass food."

"I guess that's cool. As long as it ain't another nigga."

"I don't know. Chef Lance is kinda cute *and* he can cook," she said, then broke out in a laugh.

"Why you trying to get that man hurt?" She laughed but I was lowkey serious.

Almost as soon as we finished our salad, Chef Lance was there to remove our plates. Just as quickly as he left, he was back with two bowls of roasted red pepper, sweet potato & smoked paprika soup. Myla looked at the soup and put a spoonful up to her nose.

"Why are you smelling it?"

"To see if it'll taste good," she replied before taking another whiff.

"You smell it to see how it'll taste?"

"Doesn't everybody?" she asked, as if was a normal thing.

"Usually, I taste it to see how it tastes."

I guess it passed the smell test and she finally put a spoonful in her mouth and moaned again.

"I did not expect this soup to taste so good, baby. Did you try it yet?"

"No. I was too busy trying to figure out what the hell you were doing."

I ate a spoonful and the soup definitely tasted better than it looked.

"We need to talk about baby names. Do you have any ideas yet?" she asked.

Myla had asked me a couple of weeks ago to think about names. I told her I would, but it slipped my mind with everything we'd had going on.

"Not really. You?"

"Do you want a junior?"

"I don't know. It's never been something that I felt I had to have. Let's toss around some names to see what we come up with."

"If our son isn't named after you, then I at least want his name to start with the letter K. Something similar to yours."

"Okay."

"What about Kolton? Or just Kole?"

I shrugged my shoulders. "Those are okay. They're so close to Kolby that we might as well name him after me."

"Then it's settled. Kolby Isaac Ross, Jr. We can call him KJ," she concluded with a proud smile.

I briefly thought about what it would be like having a junior. "That's cool. What about my baby girl?"

"You think it should start with a K, too?"

"Naw, maybe an M. Something similar to your name. What about...Mykha? Or Mylan?"

"Mylan is too close to mine. I kinda like Micah? How would we spell it?"

"M-Y-K-H-A."

"I like that. We need a middle name."

"Let's use yours. Mykha Rae Ross."

She frowned her nose but before she could tell me her thoughts, Chef Lance came to retrieve our soup bowls. He came right back with the main course, which was baked lamb chops, twice baked potatoes, and a vegetable medley. It smelled good as hell.

"Can I get you two anything else before I begin to clean the kitchen?"

I looked at Myla and she was already eating. "I think we're good. Thanks."

"Baby, I've never had lamb chops before. Never even thought about ordering them at a restaurant. Lance did his thing with these. They are so tender and moist. Make sure you keep his number. I may need him to show me how he made this."

She took another bite, closed her eyes, let her head fall back, and released a moan.

"It's Chef Lance. You don't know him well enough to call him Lance and ain't gon' be no private lessons. I'll get you a cookbook."

She came out of her food trance and looked at me. "You are so jealous."

"Call me whatever you want."

"Be quiet and eat your food."

She watched me as I ate a piece of the lamb chop. It literally melted in my mouth.

"You can moan too, baby. You know it's moan-worthy."

She thought she was funny but I refused to moan about this man's food. I shook my head and continued eating. Suddenly, I had a thought and I needed to talk to Chef Lance before he left.

"I'll be right, baby. I gotta, umm, give Chef Lance a tip. These lamb chops are delicious."

"I told you!" she said to my back as I went to the kitchen. After speaking with Chef Lance, I returned to the dining room and Myla's greedy ass was almost done with her food.

"You never answered, but from your expression, I'm assuming you don't like Rae."

"I like it but it sounds funny with Ross."

"How do you feel about Myla Rae Ross?"

"How—huh? What did—"

I reached into the inside pocket of my suit jacket and pulled out the little Tiffany blue box. Pushing my chair back, I slid down to the floor, getting on one knee. Already, tears were streaming down her cheeks and her hand covered her mouth in disbelief

"How do you feel about becoming Myla Rae Ross? Baby, I don't have a special speech planned and I almost punked out a few times. We've never discussed marriage and I don't know how you feel about it. All I know is how I feel about you, baby. I want to spend the rest of my life with you. Will you marry me?" I opened the box.

She nodded her head frantically as she said, "Yes, baby. Yes, I'll marry you."

MYLA

For the past three weeks, I'd been on cloud nine. I had absolutely no idea that Kolby was thinking about proposing. We'd never had a conversation about marriage, and honestly, it wasn't on my radar. I was definitely caught by surprise. Too bad my ring finger is too fat to show off the beautiful two-carat solitaire diamond he chose. For now, it hung from my neck on a gold chain.

Apparently, Kolby had been thinking about proposing for a little while. He'd spoken to my mother and Myles about it before we left Seattle, although at the time, he didn't know when he would pop the question. So, when I called them to tell them the news, their response was, "Finally."

Surprisingly, Kolby hadn't shared with anyone else that he planned to asked me to marry him. His brothers and parents, as well as my girls, were just as surprised and excited as I was. He had Chef Lance record the whole thing, and we sent the video to the family the next morning.

Today was our coed baby shower. My mother and Myles had flown in yesterday afternoon. Mommy stayed in the guest room but

Myles wanted to find some Chicago pussy to get into, so he declined my invitation to stay at our house. Kolby and his brother had taken him out last night and Kolby got in late. He smelled like liquor and cigars. Ugh! I almost made his ass sleep on the couch.

The last few days were unseasonably warm for Chicago. By that I meant that is wasn't below freezing. To make it even better, I saw the sun seeping through the blinds in our bedroom. I sat up slowly, causing Kolby's arm to slip off the side of my stomach. Normally, that simple movement would have awakened him. However, his drunk ass was dead to the world, today.

When I came out of our bathroom after taking a shower, Kolby was still asleep. I found a pair of leggings and struggled to put them on. I knew when the babies arrived that it wasn't gonna be easy taking care of them, but I was tired of being pregnant. I wanted my body back. After putting on one of his T-shirts, I was about to leave the room when I heard Kolby's voice.

"Where you goin', baby?" he mumbled.

"To make some breakfast. I'm hungry."

"No, I got it," he offered. He prided himself on making breakfast for me, and even learned to make box pancakes.

He slowly sat up, wiping his eyes, then rubbing his temples.

"I'm good. I don't want you looking all crazy during the baby shower because you decided to get drunk last night."

"Shhh. Why you yelling?" he asked, still holding his head.

"I'm not yelling!" I yelled before leaving the room. "You got a damn hangover. Go back to sleep."

He didn't even fight me on it because he knew he needed to have himself together before the baby shower started. When I got to the kitchen, Mommy was already there, prepping to make breakfast.

"Hey, Mommy." I kissed her on the cheek as she leaned in, allowing me access.

"Hey, My. You feeling okay this morning?"

Last night, I had some major Braxton-Hicks contractions. For a minute, I thought it was time for the babies to come. Braelynn and Jaelynn were here hanging out too, and were ready to call the ambulance right along with me. Thank God Mommy was here because we definitely would have, otherwise.

"I feel good. Still felling those Braxton-Hicks occasionally. I'm a little annoyed with Kolby but it's whatever."

"Why? Was he out too late?"

"No, I don't care about that. I'm annoyed because he's still drunk and has a hangover. He knows the shower is today and he won't be fully present."

She laughed. "He's a man. Drunk or not, he wouldn't be fully present. It's a baby shower; and although, they are his babies too, most men don't care about stuff like this."

I eased down into the chair at our kitchen table. "He's not like other men, Mommy. I think he's been more excited about the babies than I have."

"Oh, I'm sure he's beyond excited about the *babies*, not the baby shower. Back in my day, men only came to load the gifts in the car. Now most baby showers are co-ed and I'm sure that is not because men pushed the issue."

"Yeah, you're probably right. I just hope his hangover is gone. He tried to get up to make me breakfast, but I told him to stay in bed."

"That's probably best. He was with your brother and you know how he can get sometimes."

Both my mom and I shook our heads at the thought. If Myles didn't know how to do nothing else, his ass could turn up. Lately he'd been trying to make some changes but he hadn't changed that damn much. Not yet, anyway.

"True."

Mommy and I continued conversing while she made breakfast, and as we ate. I sent Braelynn and Jaelynn a text telling them that Mommy had made a big breakfast; they arrived, as we were finishing up.

"Are Kyree and Kam hungover like their brother?"

"Kyree is sick as hell," Braelynn answered first. "I told him to be careful drinking with Myles but he didn't listen."

"I didn't see Kamden. He was still asleep in his room when Brae came to pick me up," Jaelynn said.

The three of us stared at Jaelynn, then looked at each other, then back at Jaelynn. Everyone knew there was something going on between them but they both continued to deny it and we couldn't find any concrete evidence that they were lying.

"You slept in separate rooms?" I asked.

She kissed her lips and shook her head. "I keep telling y'all that Kam and I are just friends. We're kinda like best friends, now that the four of y'all are getting married and having families," she explained.

Oh damn! Braelynn and I gave each other a look. I'm not sure about her, but I hadn't given much thought about both of us leaving Jaelynn behind in Seattle. Neither of us have been gone too long but I could see how it would be an adjustment for her.

"Jae," Braelynn said as she went to pull her into a hug. "I'm sorry, sis. I'll do better with communicating with you. I know it's different not having us there."

"Yeah, Jae. I'll do my best to stay in touch about things other than business. I actually wanted to asked if you would consider coming to stay with us for a few weeks after I have the babies. Like, after Mommy leaves."

"You know I gotchu," Jaelynn agreed.

"So, tell me this," Mommy said. "You aren't even attracted to Kamden. That's one attractive young man."

"Of course, Auntie Dee. I'm not blind or crazy. Kamden is beautiful. We've acknowledged that we are attracted to each other. After the bad break-up I had, I'm not ready for a serious relationship, nor want to be friends with benefits. So, we're just cool."

"I guess."

"Okay."

"If you say so."

The three of us answered simultaneously. I guess if they were meant to be together, it would happen eventually.

WE HIRED a decorator for the baby shower and she did an amazing job. The green and yellow décor was beautiful and I couldn't be happier. She incorporated KJ and Mykha's names into all of her designs and I loved it all.

The shower was in full swing. Mommy, Ms. Stella, Braelynn, and Jaelynn were in charge of everything. Kolby and I just had to show up. Right before we left, those damn Braxton-Hicks contractions started up again. Not to mention, Kolby's ass was on my nerves. He had sobered up some, but was still kind of out of it. On the way to the place we'd rented for the shower, we had a little spat.

"I can't believe you got drunk the night before our baby shower."

"My bad, baby. The shit kinda snuck up on me. It's not like it's our wedding."

"Wow! So, because it's not our wedding, it's not a big deal?"

"Myla, that's not what I said, baby. Everything will be fine. I'm good."

"I told you before you left not to let Myles get you fucked up. All you had to do was listen."

"I know, My. It's been a minute since I've been out with my brothers. We wanted to show Myles a good time and we had a lot to celebrate. Yeah, we got a little carried away. It's not the end of the world. Don't let this mess up our day. Okay?"

I didn't answer right away but eventually, I replied, "Fine."

However, I was still annoyed. He was even more touchy-feely than normal because he knew I wasn't really fucking with him. I managed to smile for all the pictures and from the ones I was shown, we looked super cute.

Most of the people at the shower were friends or family of the

Ross's. Auntie Lynn and Uncle David, Braelynn and Jaelynn's mom and uncle, along with our friend Tori, flew from Seattle. Tori being there was a complete surprise, but she'd always been cool like that.

After leading us in a few games, our hostesses announced that it was time to bless the food. Mr. Isaac led the prayer. Thankfully, it was short and sweet. Kolby and I had our own small table at the front of the room and we'd eaten when we first arrived. I was starving and Kolby needed to put something on his stomach to aide him in sobering up. His hand rested on my thigh as he talked to one of his cousins whose name I'd already forgotten.

"Why you ain't call me last night, cuz? I heard y'all kicked it hard," his cousin said.

"It was kinda last minute. My wife's brother is in town and we wanted to show him a good time. That nigga got us drunk as fuck."

His wife. He'd been calling me that since he proposed. Every time he said it, chills went through my body. In this moment, it also softened me up a little and helped me lose my attitude towards him.

"Y'all going out again tonight?" his cousin asked.

"We might. I gotta see how I'm feeling after this."

I got up to use the bathroom and his hand slipped off my thigh. He immediately reached for my hand and stopped me from walking away.

"Where you going, baby?" he asked.

"To the bathroom."

"Aye, I'll get up with you later, cuz. Let me go help my wife." His cousin nodded and walked away.

"I'm good, baby. I'll have Brae or Jae come with me."

"You sure? I can—"

"Kolby, wow! It's been years."

We both looked in the direction of the woman that had interrupted him. My eyes roamed her fit, curvy body, and when I got to her face, I was impressed by the dark-skinned beauty.

"Chelle?"

"Yes! It's me. You look...amazing," she said. I could see the hitch in her breathing as she took him in.

"Damn! I barely recognized you." He released my hand and pulled her into a...very friendly hug. "What are you doing here?"

"My mom and I saw your mom at the grocery store a couple of days ago and she invited us. I had no idea that you were umm...in a serious relationship until I saw the video on Facebook. Kinda of... shocking, honestly."

He took my hand in his again. "Aye, when you know you know. This is my wife—"

"You guys are married already?" I didn't miss the disappointed look on her face.

"Engaged, but in my mind, she's my wife. Baby, this is Nichelle. Chelle, this is Myla."

Hesitantly, I stuck my hand out and she gave me this weak-ass handshake. Neither of us said anything.

"Baby, I'll get Brae or Jae to come with me. I'll be right back."

I expected him to do as he was initially about to do and come with me, but no, the nigga said, "Okay."

As I waddled away, I heard her say, "Marriage and kids. I never thought you'd turn in your playa card. We definitely should get together before you're under lock and key."

I almost turned around and clocked her ass right in her beautiful-ass face, but I really had to use the bathroom and I actually did need help. The outfit that they chose for me was a black one-piece catsuit. I wore a long multi-print sweater over it, and a pair of black boots. The zipper for the catsuit was in the back and I couldn't reach it.

"Brae, come help me get this thing off. I need to pee."

"Who the hell is that bitch all up in Kolby's face?" was the first thing she said.

"Her name is Nichelle but I don't know who she is, exactly.

Let's go, before I—oh shit!" I looked down and didn't see anything but I felt fluid running down my legs.

"My, what's wrong?"

"Oh my God! I think my water broke!"

She looked up at me and screamed, "Koolbbyy!"

KOLBY

To say that I was shocked to see Nichelle at our baby shower would be an understatement. We grew up in the same church and had always been friends. While we were in college, we were both home for break and ran into each other at a party. That was the first time that I had ever felt an attraction towards her. She had really blossomed into a beautiful woman the first couple years of college, not that she was ever ugly.

We ended up hooking up and continued to do so whenever we were home for break. At one point, she brought up being in an exclusive relationship and I used our distance as an excuse. I attended Clark Atlanta University and she attended Southern Illinois University. That seemed to work until we both graduated and came home. When she brought it up again, I had to be straight with her and tell her I had no interest in being with her or anyone else, exclusively. Of course, she was pissed and stopped fucking with me, altogether. This was the first time I'd seen her since way back then.

"Marriage and kids. I never thought you'd turn in your playa card. We definitely should get together before you're under lock and key."

"I'm already under lock and key. If my wife doesn't mind, we can meet you for lunch or dinner sometime in the future, maybe after the twins are born."

"I was thinking, maybe just me and you." She attempted to touch my chest but I grabbed her wrist and pushed it away.

"That's definitely not gon' happen."

"Why? You don't trust yourself?" she said, coyly.

"I most definitely do, but I would never disrespect my wife by meeting up with somebody I used to fuck."

"Why do you keep calling her your wi—"

"Koolbbyy!" I heard someone scream.

I looked around the room to see where the voice was coming from and spotted Braelynn standing with Myla. A small crowd began to form around them, so I had to push my way through. When I reached Myla, she had a panicked look on her face.

"Baby, what's wrong?"

"I think my water broke."

"Oh shit!"

From that point on, I was on autopilot. I swooped her up bridal style and weaved my way through our guests. I could hear voices calling out to me, but I only had one thing on my mind, and that was getting Myla to the hospital.

Once I got her securely in the back seat of my truck, I saw that her mother had hopped in on the other side and Myles was already in the front seat.

"Are you in pain, baby?"

"No, I'm okay."

I kissed her forehead and then her lips. "I love you, baby."

"I love you, too."

When I got in the driver's seat, I gave my phone to Myles and had him called Dr. Quincy to let her know that we were on our way. I drove to the hospital in record time, and there were nurses waiting for us with a wheelchair at the emergency room entrance. By the time they got us checked in and into a room, I was nervous as hell.

"Okay, Myla. Your water bag has indeed ruptured and you are in active labor," Dr. Quincy told her.

"But I still have two more weeks before I'm full-term. Are the babies gonna be okay?" Myla asked. I could tell that she was worried.

"The twins' organs are fully developed and in place, but I'm going to give you a dose of steroids to make sure their lungs are strong. Don't worry. Everything is fine and you are right on schedule."

"Okay."

"You're already five centimeters dilated and it's too late for an epidural. Have you been having contractions?" Dr. Quincy asked.

Myla looked up at me before she responded. "Well, umm, last night and some today. I thought they were Braxton-Hicks."

"You've been having contractions?" I asked and she replied with a nod.

"It sounds like they were the real deal and you were in the beginning stages of labor. Let's pray that you continue to progress and there will be no need for a C-section. I'll be back shortly to check on you."

Dr. Quincy was gone as quickly as she had come in. Leaving the two of us alone.

"Baby, why didn't you call me last night and tell me you were having contractions?"

"I didn't know they were real. Mommy and my girls were there, so it was fine."

"I would've come home."

"You were probably already good and drunk by the time they started. How could you have helped?"

She had a point, and I could tell that me getting drunk last night really bothered her. At this stage of her pregnancy, it was irresponsible of me. Had she gone into labor last night, I would have been no good to her.

I brought her hand up to my mouth and kissed the back of it.

"I'm sorry about last night but I'm here now. You ready to meet our babies?"

"Been ready."

Kolby Isaac Ross, Jr. was born at eleven twenty-five p.m. on January 22nd, weighing five pounds and six ounces. His baby sister, Mykha Rae Ross was born ten minutes later, weighing five pounds even. Both of them were twenty inches long. By the grace of God, they didn't have to spend any time in NICU and were doing amazingly well, just like their mama.

Everything happened so fast. I thought that Myla's labor would be easy. She'd unknowingly been in labor for a whole damn day and was functioning normally. By the time we got to the hospital, she was only experiencing mild pain and was already five centimeters dilated. However, that shit changed real fast.

There were a few times when I didn't know if I would make it. Seeing her in that much pain broke me in ways that can never be repaired. My love for her grew exponentially, and I wanted to make her my wife right then and there. If a man can watch his woman give birth to his seeds and not worship the ground she walks on from that moment forward, he's not a man at all.

Finally, everyone was gone and Myla had fallen asleep. As I paced the room, holding the twins in my arms, they both looked up at me with eyes that looked just like mine. I couldn't imagine a better feeling in the world. Less than a year ago, I didn't think I was capable of a love like this. Then, out of nowhere, Myla came into my life and she was so easy to love and I wouldn't change a thing.

EPILOGUE

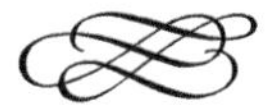

Six Months Later

Myla

Motherhood was no joke, but I loved every second it of it. Six months had gone by and I finally felt as if I had a handle on being a working mother of twins. The first two months, even with all the help I had, I didn't know if I would make it. Breastfeeding two growing babies at the same time was a full-time job, and I felt like a cow because all they did was eat. But my snap back was all that and I was proud to say that I looked better than I did pre-baby.

Kolby was a blessing. He embraced fatherhood in a way that I've only seen on T.V. Every time I saw him with our babies, my heart swelled and my love for him soared. He still works from home two to three days a week and spent a few hours every other Sunday going over the books for *K and B's Auto Shop*.

MyLynn's Bedroom Boutique continued to thrive. Braelynn and I continued to maintain our roles, even with our added responsibilities, and Jaelynn is always willing to step up when things got a little crazy for us. Braelynn and I decided to give her a bonus each quarter, from our own earnings, because she does such an amazing job when our lives become overwhelming.

After a busy Saturday, I had just put the twins down and was about to turn in myself. Kolby had been on his laptop for a large portion of the day, taking a break to bathe the kids, then giving them back to me to feed and put to bed. I had just gotten out of the shower and he rushed into our bedroom.

"November 22nd," he said.

"November 22nd?" I repeated.

"That's our wedding date."

"Oh, I, umm..."

"Monday morning, we're going to get our wedding license. Tuesday, we're getting married at the courthouse. On November 22nd, we're having a destination wedding in Belize...where it all started."

"Okay, baby. Let's do it."

How could I not love this man, when he made it so easy?

THE END

AFTERWORD

Dear Readers

Thank you for reading Myla and Kolby's love story. I hope you enjoyed. I had no idea that their story needed to be told and I'm glad I listened to my characters and readers. If you could please leave a review on Amazon and/or Goodreads, I would greatly appreciate it. Until next time.

Kay Shanee

LET'S CONNECT!

You can find me at all of the following:

Reading Group: Kay Shanee's Reading Korner – After Dark
Facebook page: Author Kay Shanee
Instagram: @AuthorKayShanee
Goodreads: Kay Shanee
Subscribe to my mailing list: Subscribe to Kay Shanee
Website at www.AuthorKayShanee.com

OTHER BOOKS BY KAY SHANEE

Love Hate and Everything in Between

Love Doesn't Hurt

Love Unconventional

I'd Rather Be With You

Can't Resist This Complicated Love

Love's Sweet Serenade

The Love I Deserve

Loving Him Through The Storm

Since the Day We Met

COMPLETED SERIES

Until the Wheels Fall Off

Until the Wheesl Fall Off...Again

Could This Be Love

Could This Be Love ~ Part 2

CPSIA information can be obtained
at www.ICGtesting.com
Printed in the USA
LVHW021540061120
670969LV00010B/1030